DIRE WOLF WANTED

ICE AGE SHIFTERS BOOK 4

CAROL VAN NATTA

CHAVANCH PRESS

Dire Wolf Wanted
(Ice Age Shifters Book 4)

Ice Age Shifters™ is a trademark of Carol Van Natta

Cover and logo design by Amanda Kelsey of Razzle Dazzle Design

Canis dirus illustration by Sam Salas

Editing by Shelley Holloway of Holloway House

Published by Chavanch Press

The magical world stands on the brink of war, unless two extraordinary shifters can bridge the gulf between them.

Dire wolf shifter and Shifter Tribunal agent **Rayne Chekal** poses as a prisoner to take down an illegal auction house that traffics in shifters. **Arvik Inuktan**, agent for the Wizard Imperium and secret mythic shifter, infiltrated the auction staff with the same mission objective.

Rayne finds him sexy as hell, but confusing. Her inner wolf says they're in the mating dance, but to her, it feels more like a flailing tumble down the stairs. Arvik finds her irresistible, smart, and gorgeous. His inner beasts say Rayne is their mate, but he realizes he must track down his dark, forgotten past if he hopes to have a future with her.

However, when the auction house falls, they open a whole new can of worms. War is coming. Separated, they must figure out what they can do to stop this, and hope the other can forgive them for the choices they're forced to make.

When Rayne and Arvik meet on the battlefield, can they overcome their differences and work together to stop the evil, or will this war engulf the magical world?

Continue the enthralling paranormal romance with Dire Wolf Wanted, the fourth book in USA TODAY bestselling author Carol Van Natta's fun, action-filled, steamy-hot Ice Age Shifters™ series.

~ ~ ~ ~ ~

Dire Wolf Wanted is a complete story with an HEA and no cliffhanger, but your reading experience will be enhanced if you've read *Shifter Mate Magic*, *Shift of Destiny* and *Heart of a Dire Wolf* first.

ALSO BY CAROL VAN NATTA

Paranormal Romance

- Shifter Mate Magic (Ice Age Shifters #1)
- Shift of Destiny (Ice Age Shifters #2)
- Heart of a Dire Wolf (Ice Age Shifters #3)
- Dire Wolf Wanted (Ice Age Shifters #4)

- In Graves Below (Magic, NM)

Space Opera - Central Galactic Concordance Series

- Last Ship Off Polaris-G (Novella)
- Overload Flux (Book 1)
- Minder Rising (Book 2)
- Zero Flux (Novella)
- Pico's Crush (Book 3)
- Pet Trade (Novella)
- Jumper's Hope (Book 4)
- Cats of War (Novella)
- Spark Transform (Book 5)
- Central Galactic Concordance Box Set Books 1-3

Retro Science Fiction Comedy

- Hooray for Holopticon

The magical world stands on the brink of war, unless two extraordinary shifters can bridge the gulf between them.

Dire wolf shifter and Shifter Tribunal agent **Rayne Chekal** poses as a prisoner to take down an illegal auction house that traffics in shifters. **Arvik Inuktan**, agent for the Wizard Imperium and secret mythic shifter, infiltrated the auction staff with the same mission objective.

Rayne finds him sexy as hell, but confusing. Her inner wolf says they're in the mating dance, but to her, it feels more like a flailing tumble down the stairs. Arvik finds her irresistible, smart, and gorgeous. His inner beasts say Rayne is their mate, but he realizes he must track down his dark, forgotten past if he hopes to have a future with her.

However, when the auction house falls, they open a whole new can of worms. War is coming. Separated, they must figure out what they can do to stop this, and hope the other can forgive them for the choices they're forced to make.

When Rayne and Arvik meet on the battlefield, can they overcome their differences and work together to stop the evil, or will this war engulf the magical world?

Continue the enthralling paranormal romance with Dire Wolf Wanted, the fourth book in USA TODAY bestselling author Carol Van Natta's fun, action-filled, steamy-hot Ice Age Shifters™ series.

~ ~ ~ ~ ~

Dire Wolf Wanted is a complete story with an HEA and no cliffhanger, but your reading experience will be enhanced if you've read *Shifter Mate Magic*, *Shift of Destiny* and *Heart of a Dire Wolf* first.

ALSO BY CAROL VAN NATTA

Paranormal Romance

- Shifter Mate Magic (Ice Age Shifters #1)
- Shift of Destiny (Ice Age Shifters #2)
- Heart of a Dire Wolf (Ice Age Shifters #3)
- Dire Wolf Wanted (Ice Age Shifters #4)

- In Graves Below (Magic, NM)

Space Opera - Central Galactic Concordance Series

- Last Ship Off Polaris-G (Novella)
- Overload Flux (Book 1)
- Minder Rising (Book 2)
- Zero Flux (Novella)
- Pico's Crush (Book 3)
- Pet Trade (Novella)
- Jumper's Hope (Book 4)
- Cats of War (Novella)
- Spark Transform (Book 5)
- Central Galactic Concordance Box Set Books 1-3

Retro Science Fiction Comedy

- Hooray for Holopticon

A rvik Inuktan tapped the icon for patient notes on his tablet as he assessed the woman on the clinic bed.

The unconscious shifter looked like something the dog dragged in. It was a distinct improvement over five days before, when she'd looked like death. Arvik smiled wryly at his own dark humor, because both comparisons were true.

Her broken, bloody body had been delivered by the auction house guard, who happened to be a force-changed wolf shifter who virulently hated all other shifters. He'd clearly believed she was dead, because he'd left her unchained on the prisoner transport cart in the hall outside the clinic without a word.

Arvik felt the spark of life even before he'd touched her.

His auction-house bosses, facility manager Aldenrud and the wizard Balton, thought they'd hired a thirty-five-year-old human academic wizard from Andorra named Arturo Muntanya de Vega Díaz. His knowledge of both technology magic and healing spells saved them the cost of hiring two people.

If they or the owners knew who they'd really hired, they

would have killed him instantly. Fortunately, they hadn't looked past the sneering, entitled, clothes-horse façade they'd all expected from his prestigious résumé and references, and his supposed need to lie low for a while owing to mundane European politics. They thought they had him pegged.

It gave him the freedom to save Rayne Chekal's life. The guards had clearly intended to end her by their savage beating. In the course of the five days and the considerable magical energy it had taken to heal her, he'd made three impossible discoveries.

First, she had more free magic than most shifters, and he'd been able to direct it to help heal her without her shifting, which should have been impossible. All shifters had superb recuperative powers, but recovering from catastrophic injuries usually took shifting to their non-injured form to heal them.

Second, he couldn't figure out her true animal form or her scent. Her records said maned wolf, with a bad photo of a tall, slender, stilt-legged wolf with a shoulder mane, but his magic said subtle illusion, which made no sense. The intake examiner had completely missed it. Her scent varied from one whiff to the next, which should be impossible. At that moment, she smelled of viburnum and granite. The auctioneer complained that customers wouldn't buy her because she smelled like rot. Arvik had studied and practiced magic all over the world but had never come across anything like it.

Third, the usually dormant and thoroughly hidden parts of him had woken up to insist she belonged to him, and he to her.

Never mind that he'd been taught that his kind weren't true shifters and couldn't have true mates. Never mind that in nearly five hundred years of living, he'd never found reason to doubt it.

Never mind that exposing his true nature would get him murdered, probably by her. True shifters hated his kind, with good reason.

Chekal's eyelids twitched. She'd exhibited increasing signs of regaining consciousness for the last half hour, and he couldn't let her see or smell him. Mating instinct might already be compromising his judgment. When the auction house unraveled, they'd each be lucky to get out alive on their own, without being a potential vulnerability to each other.

He closed his tablet without making any notes, then pulled back the sheet so he could wrestle her floppy limbs into the unisex sweatpants and T-shirt that constituted the prisoner uniform. He might not be able to acknowledge her existence, but he'd be damned if he'd leave her undressed for the guards to ogle. Shifter indifference to nudity still titillated some of them.

He lifted her and placed her gently on the cart, arranging her limbs to look as if he'd shoved her onto it. Attaching the cart's shackles and chains to her ankles and wrists took but moments. Rather than add the chained, charmed collar, he used magic to render it unrepairable, as he'd done with any cart he got his hands on. Maintenance— and morale—in the facility were at all-time lows.

He brushed her wavy dark bronze hair back and memorized her beautiful brown face, which had faint laugh lines visible even when she slept. He allowed himself one long moment to imagine a different life path. Strolling in sunlight, instead of sneaking in shadows, with a smiling woman by his side.

He stood, grinding his teeth, sliding into his perpetually prickly persona, Arturo Muntanya de Vega Díaz, the man the world owed recompense for being forced to live in an underground compound full of low-life shifters and small-minded guards. Arturo might be stuck in a menial job for the time being, but he was destined for better things than illegal auction houses that sold kidnapped shifters and other magical creatures to unscrupulous buyers.

Arvik clomped down the administrative wing hallway in his heavy boots, pulling the wheeled cart behind him. Cracks and dust everywhere gave mute testimony to the strength of the earthquake four days ago that changed everything and sped up his timetable.

All the fairies, elves, and other ancient-race captives, and easily three-quarters of the shifters, had taken advantage of the damaged cells and ruptured magical spells to escape. The hunters only recaptured about fifteen shifters. Aldenrud and Balton hastily moved up the date of an exclusive cash-only collectors' sale to get top dollar for the remaining inventory before word got out.

Despite a memo from the executive board declaring they'd build again elsewhere, Arvik knew the business was fatally wounded. Not even Aldenrud, with his fabled financial-turnaround specialist skills or the powerful wizard talents of Magister Balton could save it.

Arvik had already alerted his real bosses about the perfect opportunity to capture not just the staff and the buyers, but the secret wizard owners, who would surely want their last crumbs of profits before scattering like cockroaches exposed in the bright kitchen light.

He stopped in front of the two guards who stood at the top of the ramp that led down to the cells. "Chekal is fixed. Where do you want her?"

Foster, the wolf-shifter guard, looked at a paper list. "Seven. I'll show you."

"Not so fast, Mister Wizard," said Perry, a slender,

sallow-faced guard with a utility belt full of weapons she toyed with a lot. "Why didn't you use the collar? She's dangerous. Nearly killed Briggs."

"Broken." He waggled his fingers and spoke as if to a toddler. "All the pretty magic leaked out."

"Policy says…" Perry's expression soured. "Oh, who the fuck cares? Go."

Arvik followed Foster and trudged down the ramp with the cart into the only prisoner wing not totally ruined by the earthquake or the subsequent flood when the underground water supply system cracked open.

A sharp-edged jangle of dissonant spells assaulted his magical senses. Magister Balton had sledge-hammered shifter-containment spells on top of the existing fairy- and elf-containment spells instead of redoing them. Arvik didn't have to feign irritation by the time he got to the cell door.

Foster put two fingers in his mouth and whistled loudly. "Walls, now!"

The eight shifters in the cell glared or snarled at him, but complied with his order to move and stand with their backs to the walls. All captives had learned the hard, painful way not to disobey.

Foster used the control panel to open the cell door, then readied a lightning rod, a baton that emitted enough amperage to stop any shifter cold and dead.

Arvik warily eyed the cell's occupants as he rolled the cart in. He recognized them all from pictures, but he'd had two of them in his clinic more than once. Mondo was the berserker gorilla shifter who goaded the guards, even though they often left him unconscious, and Lerro was the crazy, palsied mysterious shifter who couldn't be forced by anyone or anything to reveal his animal.

Privately, Arvik couldn't imagine why Lerro was still alive. The guards had to shoot him with tranquilizer darts just to get him to the auction block without a vicious fight, and no one was buying.

Arvik removed the shackles. He sent a wordless apology that Chekal would never get, then unceremoniously rolled her off the cart onto the floor.

Foster whistled again for attention and thumped the lightning rod against the heel of his hand. "Don't damage her, or we'll fry you."

Arvik took the cart without a backward glance, using the reflection in the opposite cell's mirror spell to watch the shifters. Everyone eyed Chekal and Foster except shuddering Lerro, who watched Arvik in the same reflection.

A wisp of subtle magic brushed Arvik's senses, even through the magic-charged atmosphere of the prisoner wing. He'd been in the spy game a long time for a variety of causes, and recognized confluence magic when he felt it. Rare and dangerous, especially if the catalyst couldn't control it, but unlikely events suddenly became more possible.

Whether it would be to his advantage, or Rayne Chekal's, or the other captives, was anyone's guess.

Foster closed the cell door and activated the mirror spell, then led the way back up the ramp to the central hub, where the spokes for the various wings intersected. Arvik followed sullenly behind.

At the top of the ramp, Arvik looked around. "Just you two on shift? What happened to the Armadillos?"

Most of the human guards were gone, either from death and injury or simply abandoning their jobs, despite the promised pay raise and cash bonus. From his snooping, he'd learned the kreshiks, the non-human, armor-plated, tusked guards, had all been pulled for a special raid in northern Canada, but he wanted to know what the remaining staff knew.

Perry shrugged. "Two died when E Wing collapsed. Rioting shifters killed Roazer during the esca..., uh, recent *blowout sale*." She rolled her eyes at the last descriptor, which management had insisted they all use.

Foster plopped himself on the stool in front of several tables and carts with mismatched security monitors. "Good riddance." He jiggled a cable in a wired hub. The facility's sophisticated control room hadn't survived what a dragon acid and an otherworld fairy portal did to it. "She started more fights than she stopped."

Arvik pushed the cart to where the others were lined up against the wall.

Perry's mouth twisted. "The rest of the Dillos got sent yesterday for some newly discovered glory prize up north." She made a disgusted noise. "Not like we needed them to catch runaways or anything."

Foster shook his head. "Might have helped if those stupid chips we had to shoot into shifter asses worked better and we caught more of the escapees. No way the goddamn Shifter Tribunal can look the other way now." Popular rumor held that the Shifter Tribunal had been paid well to ignore the auction house's activities.

Arvik wiped his hands with his white linen handkerchief, which he carefully folded when he was done. "How very like this place not to have tested them regularly."

When he'd discovered that fact, he'd taken advantage of it to destroy the spell-laden chips in himself and every captive he healed. He'd removed Rayne's altogether. The rest of the staff could fend for themselves.

Foster made a derisive noise. "You got that right."

Arvik pocketed his handkerchief, then turned and clomped away toward the clinic. Arturo Díaz, talented wizard destined for greatness, was done talking to know-nothing guards.

The hidden parts of him mourned their separation from the magical shifter female they'd claimed as their own. He shut himself off from the distraction. Arvik Inuktan, elite agent of the Wizard Imperium, had a raid to plan, and less than six hours to do it.

From the painful stiffness in every single square inch of her, Rayne Chekal guessed she'd been run over by a tank at least twice. Maybe five or six times, just to be sure. Even her eyelids hurt.

The scent of too damn many shifters brought memories flooding back. She'd awakened on the floor hours ago, disoriented, and made the mistake of trying to stand.

A shifter named Lerro had been there to catch her, though he shook with tremors and seemed hardly able to stay upright himself.

She'd barely made it to a mattress pad that smelled of him before exhaustion mugged her and took her down for the count.

Now, she uncurled from her ball and pushed herself upright to gauge her surroundings. Eight shifters, three of whom she'd been in cells with before. Most of them flawed in some way that made them damaged merchandise. As far as the auction house knew, she was equally flawed, thanks to her layered illusions that discouraged buyers. Her true inner wolf, quiet and still healing, stayed well hidden.

The magic in the cell bars felt wrong. She wasn't a genius with magic like her younger sister, but she had a finely tuned instinct for discord.

Lerro, the palsied shifter who she'd seen before but had never shared a cell with, half-sat and half-collapsed next to her on the pad, then offered her a bottle of water.

Nodding her thanks, she drank half of it in one draught. Her stomach gurgled and cramped. She pasted a bright smile on her face. "So, did anything exciting happen while I was dead?"

Lerro and the others brought her up to speed.

The nearly fatal fight she'd started with the guards had been five days ago. Four days ago, an earthquake damaged most of the complex, leaving only one usable prison wing. The administrative and auction wings had unfortunately survived. Most of the prisoners escaped. The managers planned to hold a quick sale of the forty or so shifters that remained, crowded into five usable cells in what was formerly the fairy wing. No wonder the magic felt weird.

Rayne didn't ask, but Lerro already seemed to know about her sister. "Skyla thought you died. We all did. She told everyone to be ready and help each other. She broke the shifter cell-door spells during the earthquake."

Rayne's eyes widened. "Did she create the earthquake?" It wouldn't entirely surprise her, given Skyla's phenomenal talent for powerful, complex magic.

A corner of Lerro's mouth twitched in what may have been amusement. "The moon goddess created it. They took advantage of her blessing."

Rayne braced herself for bad news. "Did Skyla make it out?"

The burn-scarred badger shifter named Chess, a former roommate, sat on the other side of her. "I saw her and Brick, the human-brain-damaged Siberian tiger, go out a hidden emergency exit before it flooded." He laughed derisively. "Blind-ass guards kept mistaking Lerro for her when they did headcounts."

How like her sister to help someone in need. Rayne held tightly to the hope that Skyla got safely away.

Rayne's scheme to get herself caught by the auction house had inadvertently snared her brilliant, gentle, younger sister, too. For that, Rayne deserved every hit, kick, and magical punch she'd taken, and especially for making Skyla think she was dead. Her sister never would have left without her, otherwise, and Rayne had an auction house to ransack for its records before destroying it for good.

Dizziness fought with nausea. The illusions she'd magically bound to her bone marrow and glands had saved her life more than once, but they extracted a price. "When's the next meal?"

The hyena shifter stress-pacing back and forth barked a laugh. "You may smell odd, but you are a true shifter." His Zulu accent and his black-as-night skin put him far from his original home. "Supper in one hour, about. They keep a regular schedule now."

When she'd first arrived, the auction house had done its best to keep their captives off-balance by varying meal times and sleep periods, and keeping the location top secret. It didn't work well on her because her strongest magical gift was discovery.

She'd memorized the guards and quickly figured out which wore watches or carried forbidden cellphones while on duty. From conversations they'd thought private, she learned that the underground facility hid in the hills above Santa Barbara, California, and that buyers flew in via helicopter. She'd made sure to tell every shifter she'd ever been in a cell with.

Although she was now stiff, she was undamaged and

cleaner than she'd been in weeks. She couldn't have healed the catastrophic damage she'd had in five days without magical help, which meant someone might have discovered some of her secrets. "Who brought me back?"

Mondo, the wide-chested gorilla shifter, missing an ear and three toes, padded over. "The jerk wizard."

Rayne laughed. "Name one that isn't."

The old capybara shifter named Octavia, sitting in the corner near the toilet and sink, chuckled. "The pretty jerk with the short beard and all the jewelry. The guards call him 'Boy Wizard' behind his back. He's the only one left besides Balton."

A tremor shook Lerro hard, raising his knees and slamming his head against the back wall.

Rayne didn't know how to help him. Even if she had enough magic reserves to cast a healing spell, all the ones she knew needed specific targets.

Lerro grabbed her arm and pulled her close to whisper in her ear. "You're off to see the wizard."

Suddenly her face slammed hard onto his knee. Pain exploded in her nose. Blood sprayed.

She rolled away, across Chess's legs and onto the floor in a defensive crouch, expecting another attack.

It didn't come. Lerro shook with his own private earthquake, in full-blown seizure. His eyes rolled up as his head repeatedly banged against the wall.

She stood and backed away, but the pain stayed with her. She used the hem of her T-shirt to stanch the blood coming from her nose and lacerated mouth. So much for being clean and healthy again.

Mondo marched to the corner, where the cell bars fronted the concrete walls, and shouted up at the ceiling camera just outside the cell. "Hey, guards!" He pointed at thumb toward Rayne. "Better get her back to the infirmary."

The guard called Foster showed up moments later with a transport cart, so they must have already seen the incident.

Foster leveled his weapon. "Hug the walls!"

Everyone except trembling Lerro followed the order.

Foster opened the cell door and shoved the cart halfway in. "Chekal, on the cart. Shackle up."

Rayne sat on the cart, swung her legs up, and locked the shackles on each ankle and wrist. She ignored the obviously broken neck restraint.

Icy *déjà vu* slid through her. She'd taken on the role of a chained and collared feral, with her animal mind in control of her human body, so her sister would believe her death. She shook the painful, guilty memory off as unhelpful. She'd need all her wits to deal with boy wizards.

Foster hauled her up the ramp. He handed her cart over to Perry, then sat at a table full of monitors.

From what Rayne could see of the hub, the gutted shell of the control room looked like something had exploded outward. Shattered and melted glass glinted in frames that had once held windows. A tangled mess of cables ran through rough-cut pipe straps nailed to the ceiling.

Perry, who had a watch and a cell phone, grumbled a litany of cursing complaints about being short staffed, double shifts, and no help from clueless bosses as she pulled the cart down the administration wing's hall.

Rayne hated riding on her back, and each bump over the uneven surface made her head thump. She couldn't smell anything but her own blood. Ordinarily, her swollen nose and bruised face would heal in under an hour, even without shifting, but not after what she'd been through.

Perry stopped the cart in the hallway and used her nightstick to pound on a door with a big white cross painted on it. "Customer for you, Díaz!"

The door opened to reveal a lithe, dark-haired man in black. A wide darkened leather bracelet peeked out from under a shirt cuff. He scowled at Perry. "You broke her *already?*" A Spanish accent threaded through his testy tone.

"Not us. She was too close to crazy-ass Lerro when he had one of his fits." Perry looked at her watch. "Do your thing fast. The auctioneer wants fresh pictures in twenty minutes."

Díaz's annoyed expression turned to exasperation. "Of course. I'll wave my star shine glitter-wand."

Perry blew out a hissing breath. "Just make her look pretty on the outside, so she starts a bidding war, so we get the percentage bonus Aldenrud promised us for staying." She took a step away, then turned back. "And for God's sake, hose her off or something. She smells like a sewer." Perry wrinkled her nose as she strode away down the hall, her equipment belt jingling.

Díaz pulled the cart into a room with three empty treatment beds and one wall lined with closed cabinets. The stinging antiseptic smell cleared her sinuses and made her eyes water. She didn't think she'd ever been there before, but it felt familiar.

Díaz slammed the door shut, then stood facing her, arms crossed, frowning. "What's the English phrase? You keep coming back like a bad penny."

Díaz's voice sounded familiar, too, even though she'd only seen him from a distance. Considering recent events, he'd probably been the one to heal her, and likely in this room. Her inner wolf nudged her to focus because she was missing something.

She rattled a chain. "Not my choice."

He stomped noisily around her cart to the counter with drawers underneath and cabinets above. He rummaged in a drawer as he turned on water in the narrow sink.

She set her intuition loose as she watched him, looking for clues as to what hid beneath the prickly surface of petulance and condescension.

She'd already noted the necklaces, multiple earrings, and wide metal wristbands with flashy gems surrounded by subtle runes. The heavy, black work boots didn't go with the rest of his attire. From the back, his charcoal silk shirt and designer black-leather pants hugged his trim and tightly muscled figure like a second skin. His slightly swarthy, intensely handsome features and dark hair and beard could be from any of a dozen ethnicities. No wonder Octavia had called him pretty.

Magic flared from him. It felt like a shielding spell of some sort. Unexpectedly, it also felt like plush velvet brushing every inch of her. Her inner wolf leaned into the sensation and sent her a suggestion. Inwardly, she rolled her eyes. *I am not licking him.*

He tossed a washrag onto the cart next to her hand. "Clean your face."

Irritated, she lifted her shackled arm and rattled the short chain.

He sighed gustily, then focused his gaze on the shackle. Magic flared. The shackle popped open, along with the one on her neck.

Her idiot inner wolf shivered with sensuous delight. Her human brain noted the easy precision of his spell. Control like that took time and practice to achieve, meaning he was likely older than the mid-thirties he looked to be. And strong, because youth spells for humans took a lot of power.

She draped the warm, soapy washrag over her mouth and chin, then gingerly pushed it around to mop up half-dried blood.

He cleared his throat. "Your magic feels depleted. Can

you shift?" She must have imagined the hint of compassion in his dark eyes before he turned his head.

Yes! barked her wolf, sending an image of a huge, orange-eyed, Arctic-white dire wolf prancing like a show pony. *He is one of us.*

Rayne needed to have a serious discussion with her furry half about its runaway imagination.

She pulled the washrag away from her mouth. "No, I can't."

While shifting would take care of the swelling and bruises, she couldn't risk him discovering her secrets. She couldn't work magic as well as a wolf. He had too many advantages already.

He frowned. "Are you sure? Quick-repair spells hurt."

She couldn't tell if he wanted to see her shift or save her pain. Either way, she didn't trust him. "Do what you have to do."

A fleeting expression that said "It's your funeral" crossed his face.

Magic flared. Her face felt like she stuck her head in a furnace. Involuntary tears formed. She recognized the spell as a variant of one she often used, but more powerful.

Her body came alive, primed, ready for action, preferably the hot-and-sweaty-in-bed kind. Her inner wolf writhed in pleasure. An unknown, enticing scent curled up into her nostrils and sent her wolf into paroxysms of bliss, and an electric jolt through her breasts and core. *Ours!*

An involuntary gasp escaped her as shock rocked her harder than a roundhouse punch from a rock giant.

This vain, condescending, slave-trading wizard, this exotically handsome man who was far older than he looked, this *hidden shifter with three spirits*, according to her own hidden wolf, was her mate.

Intellectually, she recognized the classic signs—the best

scent in the world, the instant hormone rush, the compatible magic that felt like foreplay. Plus the enticing subtle golden glow of drifting mate-bond threads, which she'd only seen for other shifters, never herself. Just like all the stories.

Rayne must have committed some horrible sin against the moon goddess.

No way was she the true mate of a freaking wizard-*shifter* who willingly profited off selling other shifters like they were sheep to a slaughterhouse. She'd just as soon kill him as kiss him. If she was feeling charitable, she'd turn him over to the Shifter Tribunal. Maybe she'd visit him in prison.

She ruthlessly dragged her eyes from him to stare at the ceiling, letting herself wince from the pain of the healing spell to cover her reaction. Distractions could kill her if she didn't focus.

The cart began to vibrate. The cabinet doors rattled in their frames and drawers jostled open. She'd lived in Los Angeles long enough to know an earthquake when she felt one. She hoped the cracked ceiling would hold, or she'd soon be Rayne pancake.

Díaz muttered a curse in Spanish as he strode toward the wide metal desk to pull the two chairs away. He waved a hand toward her.

All her shackles snapped open. She rolled off the cart and into a crouch on the shaking floor.

He crouched down and under the desk. "Get under here."

She narrowed her eyes at the peremptory command but followed his order. Standing on principle was a good way to become an earthquake casualty. Crouching under the sturdy desk upped her survival odds, but it put her closer to him than she liked.

The ground shaking subsided after a dozen seconds, so it was likely just an aftershock. Unfortunately, it was plenty of time to memorize his unique human scent, the one he hid under a veneer of prickly wizard magic and something icy cold and darker than night.

Just fucking fabulous. Her prize of a would-be mate also dabbled in black sorcery.

Maybe she'd sinned against a whole pantheon of gods.

She was consoling herself with the fact that he obviously didn't feel anything toward her but irritation, when she noticed perspiration beaded on his face and his clenched jaw, and his eyes momentarily flashed red-gold.

Fear washed away the tendrils of desire and raised the hackles of her inner wolf. She lunged out and away from him fast, giving herself room.

Meeting a true mate was supposed to be blessed and magical, but every shifter knew the whispered tales of bad and tragic matings. True-mate biology affected ferals and sociopaths, too.

If he lost control with her, she wasn't going down without a fight.

3

A rvik's jaw ached with the effort to keep the Arturo Díaz shell from shattering.

Even if he still didn't know Rayne Chekal's true scent, he felt everything else his mated shifter friends had talked about—desire, fascination, protectiveness, hope. His secret inner beasts not only didn't care about the immediate danger and impossible situation, they wanted to meet her and tell her everything.

He watched her spring away from him and felt her unique shifter magic surge. Not alpha, not loner, just different. Compatible with his own, just like mates should be. He'd always been a sucker for learning new magic.

She will heal us, his beasts asserted.

He wasn't damaged, and Arvik didn't have time to wonder what they were talking about. *She's scared*, he told them. *She'll kill us.*

Most shifters had speed and fight experience, but she had lethal skills that didn't come from ordinary pack life. In between healing sessions, he'd watched the security video of her fight with the guards. Feral or not, it had taken eight of them to bring her down. He wouldn't have lasted as long, even with magic.

He slowly stood, then sidled away from her and held up his hands in a show of peace. "I swear that I will not harm you."

The scorn in her bark of laughter could etch glass.

He deserved it. Considering she likely thought of him as a slaver, it had been a useless thing to say, even if it was the truth.

He gave her one of Arturo's put-upon sighs. "I have to take you back." He pointed to the cart.

She raised a pointed eyebrow, then sat on the cart. She kept an eye on him the whole time as she attached the shackles to her ankles and wrists. Somehow, she managed to make each snap remind him of his pledge not to harm her.

He needed a long vacation after this mission. Fine food. Dark forest. Ocean beach. An adventurous lover. A slender, long-legged maned wolf to play with in the snow—

The clinic door slammed open with a loud bang.

Arvik cast an aggrieved glare at the facility manager, Aldenrud, who stood in the doorway. "By all means, barge right in."

Aldenrud, a sorcerer who had cultivated a corporate middle-manager look, down to artfully graying temples and an old-school tie, was impervious to Díaz's sarcasm. He looked over Chekal with assessing eyes. "She'll do. Take her straight out. The executive board is making an unannounced visit and wants to see all the shifters."

Arvik very much wanted to see the board, but it wasn't wise to let his surprise or eagerness show. He raised his eyebrows. "Chained to the cart?" A distinct breach of the auctioneer's rules. Buyers wanted healthy shifters who stood on their own two feet.

Aldenrud tightened his lips in annoyance. "No, find some walking shackles or chains. Just get her out there."

Aldenrud turned and exited, leaving the door wide open.

Arvik turned to find her watching him expressionlessly. She probably killed at bluff games. Maybe he could challenge her to a game of strip poker, so he could lose on purpose.

He gave himself a mental shake. Mating instincts were not helping. Secret missions took precedence over desire-driven thoughts.

With luck, his hasty shield spell kept her from recognizing him as her mate, assuming she even felt the call. Despite the stubborn insistence of his nagging animals and the sudden tightness of his pants when near her, he wasn't convinced he felt the call, either.

He reseated himself in Arturo Díaz's grumbly skin and pushed Chekal on the cart to the hub, only to find it deserted. No captives, no guards, no wizards. They must all be in the auction wing.

It'd be the perfect opportunity for spying, if he didn't have Chekal. On the other hand, she was the perfect excuse.

He cast a quick spell to open the cart's shackles, then tossed sets of separate ankle and wrist shackles to her. He took the opportunity to sabotage the other sets with his magic. He detested them.

He used the looped chain on her wrist shackles to lead her into the administrative wing, then turned left into the branch with offices. He knocked confidently on the executive boardroom's ornate door, then cast a tiny spell to unlock it as he let himself in. Motion-sensor lights tripped on as he pulled her in and shut the door.

The lushly appointed room featured a two-section Georgian antique table and chairs, a fine Persian carpet, built-in bookcases full of dusty books and bookends, and gruesome trophy heads of big game animals. Staff rumor claimed they were shifters, but from their smell, they were composited fakes.

He locked the door with a flick of magic and froze the surveillance cameras, so all they'd see and hear was impatient Arturo, arms crossed, foot tapping, and a brown-skinned female shifter in chains, looking at the floor. He doubted anyone reviewed the footage, much less monitored the room in real time, but skipping little details got agents in trouble.

He left Chekal standing while he quickly went around the double-pedestal table to the cabinet that hid the wet bar and opened it. He tried the small bathroom and its shallow supply closet, but no luck. No residual portal magic.

The executive board arrived without warning, so they had to have used a hidden stable portal. He'd have felt the power from a temporary portal or personal transport spell. He'd detected no fixed wizard portals in the facility, but he was nearly blind to fairy magic unless he used elven magic, which left traces he couldn't afford. This was the only room he hadn't been in.

"Nothing worth stealing?" She leaned one shoulder against the wall. Her tone was half taunt, half curiosity.

He frowned. Arturo didn't like smart-mouthed shifters. Arvik didn't want her to think even worse of him than she already did. He edged around the table, closer to her. "I'm looking for the way in."

He only saw her eyebrow twitch because he was mesmerized by her intelligent brown eyes flecked with gold. Awake, she was even more stunning than when she'd been a sleeping beauty. He'd avoided her gaze until then for just that very hazard.

She pushed herself off the wall. "Trade you. I can find hidden things."

He dragged his eyes away from her to glance at the door and the ornamental clock on the wall. "What do you want—your freedom?"

Our mate will see us, said his animals. He shushed them, since they weren't making sense. He got a whiff of wet wool and copper. Her scent wasn't making sense, either.

"Pfffft," she said dismissively, then caught his eye. "Sales records."

Unrelated facts snapped into place. He'd been so distracted by the endgame, her electrifying presence, and his suddenly loquacious animals, he'd nearly missed it. Rayne Chekal was an agent.

Considering she was an extraordinary shifter with magic... "You're with the Shifter Tribunal."

She cocked her head and gave him a speculative look. A corner of her mouth twitched. "You're with the Wizard Imperium?"

Trust her, demanded his animals.

He hesitated, then nodded. He hoped to hell his animals were right.

She blew out an exasperated breath that lifted a lock of her hair. "Just once, would it hurt the magical-world policing agencies to fucking *talk* to each other?"

He smiled wryly. "And admit to the others they have a problem?"

His plans were already in motion, but he could still help her. "Aldenrud has two sets of books, one just for him. Are you looking for names or money?"

"Names. What's your target?"

"The true owners." He smiled lopsidedly. "They're behind on their dues." The North American Wizard Imperium deserved its former reputation for tolerating any wizard project as long as it didn't endanger the secrets of the hidden world of magic and the Imperium got a percentage. He wouldn't be working for them if they hadn't mostly cleaned up their act.

She smiled briefly in response, then pointed to the far wall where trophy heads surrounded a museum-sized oil painting of a landscape view out a window. "Illusion of a portal. Feels like it's armed and alarmed." She pointed to the table. "That pulls apart. It's a dormant fairy portal. I've seen one like it."

A noise in the hall galvanized him. He broke open her shackles with a flick of power. "Can you leave via the portal?"

"Don't know where it goes. Besides, not without the records." Her expression said he'd waste his breath trying to persuade her.

It didn't make him happy that she wouldn't be safe, but he respected her choice. Not that she'd appreciate or trust his unexpectedly strong protective impulse. "We have forty-five minutes. My people are among the buyers."

"What about the executive board?"

"Not my people." He frowned. "I thought they were a paper fiction for the dummy corporation."

She tilted her head. "Then we'd better go see them before they come looking for us." She bent to scoop up both sets of shackles. "Can you make it so I can open these?"

"Yes. Do you have backup?"

She held out the ankle shackles. "These are cool. Can I keep them?"

He shrugged. "They're not tracked anymore." Before he could ask what she intended, she shifted into a tall, slender, big-maned wolf that had no remnants of clothes on its body. It only took seconds. Moments later, she shifted back equally quickly, again wearing the blood-stained T-shirt and sweats. She held the wrist shackles, but the ankle shackles were gone.

He struggled to ignore the sensual effects of her wave of unusual magic. Warm and addicting, a lover's hand caressing him as intimately as an ocean current. "I've never seen anyone shift so fast, except maybe birds."

"I'm a slug compared to my sister." She snapped the shackles onto her wrists.

He flicked his magic over them. "Tap them together three times fast, and they'll spring open."

A distant shout from the hallway spurred him into action. He pulled himself into the persona of disgruntled, stick-up-his-ass Arturo. Grabbing the lead chain from Rayne's shackles, he opened the boardroom door, then stomped out of the room with Rayne, pulling the door shut.

Just in time, because the guard named Perry rounded the corner. "What are you doing here?"

"Leaving," declared Arvik-as-Arturo. "Aldenrud said to bring her to the executive board, but I've got better things to do than stand around for hours with a barely-conscious shifter waiting for them to show up."

"You were supposed to take her to the auction wing." Perry keyed the microphone on her shoulder and spoke into it. "He's at the boardroom door with Chekal. Says you told him to go there."

She listened a moment through her earbud, then nodded. "On our way." She tapped her microphone again, then glared at Rayne's ankles. "Where are the rest of her shackles?"

Rayne's dazed expression matched the sagging exhaustion in her shoulders and slumped posture. Good, she'd taken his hint.

"Those are all I could find that worked." He waved in the direction of the prisoner wing and poured on the sarcasm. "I'm sure Aldenrud and the board will wait with patience while you show me where the extra sets are stored." He held out the lead chain to her.

Perry backed away, shaking her head. "Keep it. I'll stay upwind." She waved a hand under her nose. "Can't you smell her?"

He curled a lip. "Shifters all smell like unwashed animals to me."

Perry laughed. "True, that."

She turned and led the way down the hall at a brisk pace.

Arvik trudged noisily behind her, pulling Rayne's chain like she was an untrained puppy, as was Arturo's habit. She undoubtedly understood the need to stay in character, but it didn't make him feel any better about it.

The air-conditioned auction hall consisted of wide aisles of luxury theatre-style seating for the buyers and a raised stage and presentation area for the merchandise.

On the stage, the twelve mobile booths for displaying the captives were clustered together at the far end, dark and empty. A ragged line of forty shifters stood in front of them across the stage, shackled together like a road-work chain gang. They'd even managed to get trembling Lerro into the room, supported by two other shifters. Fresh blood stained the front of his T-shirt.

Arvik buried unbidden dark memories of mid nineteenth-century slave blocks, when he'd bought slaves with abolitionist money to send them on the underground railroad. At the time, he'd felt superior because at least he wasn't as bad as humans. Then he'd stumbled across a ring of multi-species shifters that trafficked in captured elves, fairies, and wraiths. He cherished no more illusions about his kind.

Aldenrud and Balton welcomed him as if they were happy party hosts, heartily directing him to hand the shifter over to the guards and then to come join them.

In the audience sat the board, three men and three women who could have posed for a stock photo for new-age corporation executives, exhibiting varying degrees of interest.

Aldenrud introduced him as "young Magister Díaz, our tech wizard."

Arvik-as-Arturo smiled with condescending pride, then maneuvered close to Balton so he could speak quietly. "They're all wearing high-powered glamours." The bland exteriors matched their equally bland names.

"Of course they are. Standard practice these days," Balton murmured, smiling patronizingly. "Can't be too careful, with a camera in every cell phone and tablet."

Arvik nodded in agreement. The only thing the hidden and ancient species of the world agreed on was that humankind wasn't even close to ready to learn about their existence. Still, it meant he'd have to figure out how to peek under the glamours without them knowing.

A black-haired white woman in a pastel pink and green suit looked up from her phone. "Is that all of them, then?"

"Yes, Ms. Gray." Aldenrud beamed at them. "Ready for the exclusive sale."

Balton leaned close to Arvik. "The shifters look like crash-test dummies. Glam them up before the buyers get here." He sketched a brief arcane symbol with his finger, meaning he wanted Arvik to use magic enhancers to make them more attractive.

A long-faced Italian-looking man introduced as Mr. Smith, who should not have listened to whoever recommended his plaid jacket, sat forward. "We've heard a disturbing allegation that you have secret mythic shifters that you plan to sell for a high price. And keep the extra profit."

Balton's jaw dropped. Arvik-as-Arturo mimicked the surprise, while trying to guess the board's angle.

"Nonsense," said Aldenrud firmly. "You've just examined the shifters we're selling. Do they seem mythic to you?"

"Prove it," demanded Smith. "Order them to shift."

Costigan, the auctioneer, came around her podium. "Certainly, Mr. Smith, as long as you take personal responsibility for controlling them once we remove the shackles so they can shift. Perhaps we should start with the gorilla, or the rhinoceros?"

Arvik assumed a suitably alarmed expression while watching to see if the board bought Costigan's bluff. No one left in the facility could force a shifter to change form if they didn't want to.

Aldenrud smiled like a used-car salesman and pointed to the giant flat display mounted on the wall. "Why don't we show you the intake photos we show to buyers?"

Smith laughed derisively. "You could be showing us pictures from the zoo."

Costigan shrugged. "Stay for the auction and track the sales."

"Oh, we intend to," said Gray, cutting off Smith. "We just wanted to see what you'd say. And we'll start by reviewing the financials and sales records." She waved limp fingers dismissively. "You can take the smelly creatures away now."

Aldenrud nodded to the five guards. They set about herding the shuffling shifters out through the double doors.

Arvik turned to follow, only to be pulled aside by Balton. "You stay here. Keep them entertained." He smiled as if he had everything in hand. "Text me if they go anywhere but the boardroom."

Balton strode away with Aldenrud before Arvik-as-Arturo could come up with an excuse to get out of the order.

All hell was about to break loose, and he was stuck babysitting the board that he'd presumed were as mythical as the supposed mythic shifters they were after.

Shifters like him. And unless he missed his guess, shifters like Rayne.

4

"Hey, Foster." Perry stood at the top of the ramp, hands on her hips. "Let's just leave 'em chained up in the corridor. It's only thirty minutes."

The three other guards had gone off after speaking with Aldenrud, who had disappeared into the administrative wing with Balton. Rayne hadn't forgotten Díaz's comment about two sets of books and wondered if Balton knew.

She stood in the back of the line, head down, shoulders slumped. No prospect of food or painkillers anytime soon, so she ignored her hollow stomach and tender nose.

The shifter in front of her, Lerro, sneezed into his cupped hands. His trembling seemed to have calmed for the moment, but he reeked of blood, old and fresh. The shifter in front of him rumbled a wordless threat to back off. The reaction spread down the chain.

"Nah." Foster continued opening the cell doors. "Buyers don't go for the prison inmate look. We have to separate them. And we still gotta feed 'em."

Rayne considered her options. Díaz, which probably wasn't his name, had thrown a wrench into her plans. As far as she could tell, all mate biology was good for was hot sex and making babies. It certainly didn't tell her if she could trust him.

The Wizard Imperium was another wrench. Oh sure, the buyer group would likely include their agents, but they might be more interested in stealing the business than delivering justice.

To be fair, Díaz might be equally wary of the Shifter Tribunal. Their history of brutality, corruption, infighting, and defending any shifter misbehavior, however heinous, was legendary. Not all that long ago, Tribunal enforcement had involved blood and fire instead of law and justice.

She stole a peek at Foster's big wristwatch as he walked by. If Díaz's timetable still held, his buyers would arrive in twenty minutes, presumably with reinforcements.

Her own reinforcements were already in the auction room, posing as the board. She felt guilty about not telling Díaz, but mate potential didn't make him an ally.

She'd be a lot more successful at ignoring her doubts if her inner wolf wasn't fretting about the supposed board member Smith's unexpected interest in mythic shifters. She didn't know the male under the illusion of a plaid-wearing wise-guy lawyer. Like most field agents, she stayed as far away from the halls of power as she could, in case "desk job" was catching.

Maybe Smith planned to offer her up to the buyers as a distraction. Dire wolves weren't mythic, they were throwbacks, but not all shifters made the distinction, and wizards probably didn't know the difference. Smith might consider her an acceptable loss for the greater objective.

Or maybe someone had betrayed Díaz. Agents, powerful wizards, and hidden three-spirit shifters probably collected more enemies than honest politicians did, and he was all three. And he would definitely be of interest to the Tribunal.

He'll be fine, she assured her agitated wolf. *He's got magic and centuries of experience.*

Before all the fireworks started, she needed to know about the defenses in the new wing. It hadn't been designed to hold shifters, and its overabundance of magic made her itchy. She sent her own magic looking for security systems.

A loud alarm on the nearby cell's control panel sounded.

Rayne tamped her magic and looked at the panel like everyone else did. Stupid to have forgotten the ubiquitous magic detection spells, which compensated for guards' inability to sense magic.

Perry swore. "This place is falling apart." She stomped down the ramp to the panel, where she pounded on it with the butt of her nightstick until the alarm stopped.

Rayne dropped her head again and finished her magical evaluation while her luck still held.

Damn. Once again, her plans weren't surviving contact with reality. The air ducts had enough explosives to implode the entire wing. Probably a leftover failsafe against the former ancient-races captives, but it would kill the shifters just as dead.

It was too early to send the "get out of jail" signal to her reinforcements, but she had no choice. She wouldn't leave the shifters to die. She triggered the spell she'd readied months ago, back when her plans seemed so elegant.

The panel beeped weakly. Perry hit it hard enough to crack the glass.

In the meantime, maybe Rayne could help the captives get to safety. When the raid started, the few remaining guards would be no match for rampaging shifters, but the new automatic weapons protecting the hub would make it a killing field. She'd counted six barrels with high-capacity ammo drums when she'd been through. She sent her magic looking for how to sabotage them.

Perry holstered her nightstick and turned to Foster. "You unhook them and get them into the cells. I'll shoot anyone who gives you shit."

She backed up the ramp and pulled out a .45 long Colt handgun with charmed ammo and a bespelled lightning rod issued to all guards. Perry compensated for her slight size by being fast and accurate with the multiple weapons she carried. "Leave the wrist shackles on. They can still eat. Save us work later."

In the hub's guns system, Rayne found what felt like a central node and took a chance to surge power to it. Lights flickered. Another alarm went off. She shook off the light-headed feeling. Nothing a week-long nap and a well-stocked all-you-can-eat buffet couldn't fix.

Foster walked back up the line and stopped in front of her and Lerro. "Ankles out."

They complied. He pulled a slender charmed rod out of his pocket, extended it, and touched it to the chain. The shackles dropped to the floor.

Foster pointed the rod toward the cell. "Go."

Before Rayne could move, a voice at the top of the ramp stopped her.

"What are you doing?" The board member introduced as Gray stood with her fists on her hips, glaring. Her tone was sharper than her spike heels.

Perry winced before smoothing her face. "Putting them in cells so we can feed them. Standard procedure." She spoke calmly, but her hand twitched on the handle of the lightning rod.

Gray shook her head. "No time. The buyers just landed. Get those leg-chains off and take them back to the auction room. Put them four to a booth if you have to."

Perry's nostrils flared as she took a deep breath. "Okay. I'll get Maxey and the oth—"

Gray cut her off. "What did you not understand about 'no time'? Get them in there immediately." She pointed to Rayne and Lerro. "I'll take these two. You bring the rest."

"Yes, ma'am." Foster held up his hands in surrender and stepped back. "They're all yours. Shackles are on the table next to the monitors if you want to use them. It's your problem if you don't." He stepped back. "Chekal, Lerro, go on up."

Gray flourished her fingers in a circular gesture. Magic sparks swirled into an image of a lightning bolt. "I'm sure they'll cooperate if they know what's good for them."

Rayne glanced at Lerro, who was focused on Gray. Lerro started up the ramp, so she followed.

As Rayne passed, Perry's face twisted with anger, but not so Gray could see it.

Gray beckoned with a curling finger, then spun smartly around and strode into the hub.

Surreptitiously, Rayne glanced up as they walked. A blackened spot in the center of the ceiling and the acrid smell of burnt plastic gave mute testimony to the damage her magic had done. She hoped it was enough.

Gray led them through the double doors into the auction area's stage. Usually, the display booths were lined up, ready to accept and display the captives, but they were still in the corner. She turned to catch Rayne's eye and Lerro's and pointed to their feet. "Stay."

Rayne's attention immediately singled out Díaz, who stood in the middle of the stage, head bowed and arms crossed, smartphone in one hand.

He turned to Gray. "You said you were just going to the powder room."

Rayne's wolf told her to find who was making him so

frustrated and impress him by biting them. *Mates like thoughtful gestures,* assured her wolf.

She kept her exasperation to herself as she checked out the rest of the room.

No staff, no guards, and only three board members, counting Gray. The space bristled with defenses, including the unique magic detection technology found throughout the facility, plus a dozen spells waiting to be triggered if the merchandise or the buyers got rowdy. She'd seen some of them in action.

Gray waved off Díaz's peevish comment. "*Someone* had to tell the guards to bring the shifters back in. Where are the records you promised? We start the audit during the auction." She squinted toward the alarmed and secure double doors at the far end, behind the audience seating. "How many buyers are waiting?"

Martinez, a tall brown-skinned woman with dark hair poofed high, looked up from the tablet in her hands. "The auctioneer said five. She's in the lobby, opening the self-serve bar for them. They expect fifteen more."

Díaz's phone vibrated loudly enough for any shifter to hear it. He flared a bit of magic as he looked down at it.

Rayne dropped her head to hide her reaction. Even from fifteen feet away, his magic felt like sexy warm breath on her neck. Interesting that it didn't set off the alarms.

Gray turned her gaze to the darkened display booths and took a few steps toward them. "How do those things work?"

Díaz's frown deepened as he rapidly two-thumbed a message on his phone. "I will go ask about that and the records."

Lerro edged close behind her. "The wizard must stay here." The tone was so soft, even her shifter ears barely heard him. "If he leaves, he dies. If he dies, we die."

The chill up her spine—her own personal truth meter—confirmed an oft-repeated rumor among the prisoners. Lerro was an oracle.

She rubbed her palms on her thighs. Vague predictions and do-this-or-die pronouncements always made her want to slap oracles silly.

Mate or not, she owed Díaz the professional courtesy he'd shown her. Tossing a quick prayer to the moon goddess, she crouched as if too tired to stand. She tapped her wrist shackles together three times, then caught them before they fell.

Smith, the third board member stood and put his hands on his waist, bending sideways in a stretch.

"No!" shouted Lerro.

Smith was suddenly aiming an enforcer's dart gun at Díaz.

Rayne instinctively launched herself toward Díaz. They bowled over, a tangle of limbs. His magic flared and wrapped around them in a shield.

As if they'd trained together for years, they rolled apart and each came up in a crouch, facing everyone else in the room. She hung on to her human form with a thread, ready to kill.

Martinez grappled with Smith, controlling his gun arm. "Stop, goddammit!"

He snarled through a half-shifted muzzle full of sharp teeth and tusks. She growled back with more than a hint of angry feline in her tone.

From the stage, Gray flared sharp witch magic. "Move, Elena!"

Martinez pushed Smith hard and arched herself backward away from him, careening off the padded seat.

Gray's bolt of power hit Smith but cascaded in a shower of sparks on an invisible barrier.

A red alarm light near one of the coffered ceiling beams began rapid blinking.

Smith growled angrily and swung his weapon toward Martinez.

From out of the corner of her eye, Rayne saw Lerro throw something. A swarm of glowing green beads slowed through Smith's shield, then landed on his skin and clothes.

Smith's growling turned to howling in pain. His face and form became fully human. He shudders overtook his body. The gun dropped.

Martinez darted in to grab the weapon with a blurry-fast movement and danced back.

Smith stumbled, scraping at the beads, which were burning through his clothes and burrowing themselves into his skin wherever they touched.

Gray whirled to glare at Lerro. "What were those?"

He gave her a feral smile. "Karma."

Rayne pushed to her feet and moved toward the double doors, confirming the sounds she'd heard. "The guards are bringing the rest of the shifters."

Díaz flared warm magic. The red alarm winked out. He pointed toward shuddering Smith. "Tell them he tried to use an unauthorized spell on the shifters. And shut him up." He bent down to pick up the dart that must have bounced off his shield. He sniffed it. His magic flared again, giving her wildly inappropriate thoughts as he dropped the dart into his chest pocket.

Rayne ran to Lerro and latched onto his arm. "Down." She pulled him with her down to his knees. "We're victims."

Gray's chin jutted out as she faced Díaz, power gathering in her palm. "Tell me why I shouldn't kill you where you stand, *slave-trafficker?*"

Díaz's stony face gave no indication of the mass of power he was raising.

Rayne focused on Gray, willing her to listen. "Because he's on our side. He saved my life." She clamped her jaw to contain what her inner wolf wanted to say. *Because he's our mate.*

Lerro's hoarse whisper that carried throughout the room iced her blood.

"Because without him, we're all dead."

5

Arvik reached for the coldest, darkest part of him as a lifeline in a sea of chaotic emotion and conflicting impulses.

Kill the shifter who tried to shoot him with lethal charmed poison. Get Rayne to safety. Find out why he'd been the target. Keep the mission together long enough to smoke out the true owners. Avoid being a pawn in Lerro's confluence magic. Kiss Rayne for protecting him. Kiss Rayne again on general principle. Would she taste different each time?

He ground his teeth so hard he heard his molars crack as he picked up the phone he'd dropped. He nearly laughed out loud when he saw the last message from Balton.

The back doors to the stage and the front doors from the buyers' lobby opened at the same time.

On the stage, the shifters began shuffling in in small groups, chained at the ankles. Foster, Perry, and two more guards carefully watched their progress.

Costigan closed the lobby doors behind her quietly. The

consummate professional, she carried her tablet and walked purposefully to the side stairs that led to her auctioneer's podium. "Magister Díaz. A word?"

Arvik-as-Arturo sullenly crossed to her side. "It's not my fault." He pointed to shuddering Smith, slumped into the theatre seat Martinez had wrestled him into. "I told him no magic in here. The rebound defense hit him hard."

She rolled her eyes, then tilted her head toward the clumps of shifters. "What are they all doing in here?"

He shrugged. "Gray brought two. I don't know about the rest." He wiggled his phone. "Balton texted me to 'stall,' and I don't know what he meant. The shifters? The board members? The buyers? The auction?"

She shook her head. "This is a complete cockup." She pointed her chin toward the buyers' entrance. "We've got ten more buyers than were on my list. I don't care what Aldenrud says, more *isn't* merrier." She turned to her state-of-the-art podium with its impressive array of controls and connected her tablet to it. "I'll line up the booths. Go tell the guards to load in the merchandise." She stabbed controls. Booths began lighting up.

He surveyed the shifters dubiously. "All forty of them? All at once?"

She blew out an explosive breath. "No, one per booth. Buyers expect discounts if we group them." She turned back to her podium. "I've put up with three years of shit from this place. I want my goddamn bonus."

He nodded as he slid the company-provided phone into his pocket and flicked his magic to block its suite of surveillance spells. Balton couldn't complain, or he'd have to admit he'd installed the suite in the first place.

After repeating Costigan's orders to Perry and the other guards, he headed toward Rayne and Lerro still sitting on their heels, faces cast down. The heavy boots he wore to remind him to walk like a clumsy human echoed louder on the raised wood floor.

Gray moved to intercept him. "Where are Aldenrud and Balton?" Accusation laced her tone.

He assumed that Gray and the others were likely Rayne's reinforcements, but Smith's actions worried him. Rayne wouldn't be the first field agent to be a casualty of internal politics.

"I don't know. Where are the rest of your board members?" He harrumphed in Arturo-like irritation. "I am a magister, not a sheep herder."

He stepped around Gray to pick up the shackles on the floor and hold them out to Rayne. "On."

She didn't meet his eyes, but her fingers brushed his as she took the shackles. The thrill electrified him.

He stepped back and put his fists on his hips. Touching her was too damn dangerously distracting.

"Up, both of you."

As they both climbed to their feet, Arvik took a chance to use his magic on Lerro's wrist shackles to make them open with three quick taps.

The red warning light near the ceiling stayed dark. The trick was to use wizard magic that didn't hit the detection threshold.

When Rayne looked up at him with a slightly raised eyebrow, he blinked one eye at her three times in succession, then glanced toward Lerro's wrists and back.

The corner of her mouth twitched.

He wondered if she felt his magic the sensuous way he felt hers. He selfishly hoped so, even if it wasn't safe for either of them.

He turned to find Gray staring at him with suspicious eyes.

Arvik gave her an Arturo sneer. "Better move, or you'll

get run over." He pointed to the booths that were rolling toward them, then turned to Rayne and Lerro. "Let's go."

He led them to the end of the line of shifters "Sit." He raised his voice. "All of you. Down."

As the shifters followed his order, Perry hustled over. "What are you doing?"

"Not that it's any of your business," he replied with a supercilious sniff, "but Balton ordered me to fix them up. It's easier if they're sitting."

Perry looked like she wanted to argue, but clamped her mouth shut with an audible clack. She went back to her post near the doors.

He started at the beginning of the line, where twelve prisoners were already unchained and waiting for the booths to stop moving. Under the cover of using magic to clean clothing and faces and heal visible cuts and bruises, he applied the three-fast-taps spell to every shackle they wore. He'd figure out how to tell them about it later.

It would be a pleasure to melt the booths to slag as they glided by, but he settled for tampering with the doors instead.

By the time he got to the end of the line, he was feeling the metaphysical burn of controlling the magic flow so it didn't trip the detectors.

Lerro rose to his knees and raised his clasped hands above him, his face tilted upward, like he was beseeching the gods. "Tap the wrist, bang the knee. The power of three shall set you free."

On the last word, he opened his eyes wide, unclasped his hands, and splayed his fingers. To humans, he probably sounded like a street-corner preacher. Shifters knew an oracle when they heard one.

Arvik's respect for Lerro deepened. Somehow, he'd not

only stayed alive, he'd stayed relatively sane despite dual gifts of confluence magic and oracular visions. It put the assault on Smith in a whole new interesting light.

Perry pulled out her lightning rod and activated it. "We don't have time for your crazy shit, Lerro."

"Don't be thick," snapped Arvik. "If you zap him, everyone on the chain goes, too." Sending a silent apology to Lerro, he cast a quick knockout spell. Lerro toppled onto Rayne. "He'll wake in a few minutes."

He shook his head as he watched Rayne struggle to get out from under Lerro's dead weight. "What does that mean, 'the power of three shall set you free'?" He used his native gift to compel just the shifters to pay attention to the words he quoted. He didn't like using charisma magic. His people had used it as a weapon, but he'd left them long ago.

Perry snorted as she re-holstered the rod. "Probably some lame shifter myth. They've got thousands of them."

At the doorway, Foster whistled softly for attention. "Incoming." He pulled open one of the doors.

The three missing board members plus Aldenrud and Balton filed in, followed by the guard called Carson who carried three folding chairs.

Aldenrud made a beeline for Costigan's auctioneer podium. The guard crossed behind him and started setting up the chairs nearby.

Balton and the board members walked around the end of the shifter line to stop in front of Arvik. The board members wore disgruntled expressions.

Balton pointed back toward the doors. "Go get three more chairs from the boardroom." Beads of moisture dotted his upper lip.

Out of the corner of his eye, Arvik saw Rayne's mouth silently form the word "no."

Arvik's instincts—and both his animals—said to trust her over Balton.

He assumed an Arturo-is-insulted look and crossed his arms. "I am a magister." He pointed his imperious chin toward Foster and Perry. "They are not."

Whatever Balton was about to say was interrupted by Costigan's voice over the speakers. "Perry, help McReady load the booths. Díaz, go stand by the lobby doors to let the buyers in, and tell the guard to take your place when you do. Ms. Martinez, you and Mr. Smith will have to give up your seats. We've got a full house. Snap to, people. Three minutes to auction."

Arvik turned and hurried toward the stairs that led to the audience before Balton could stop him. He saw Gray helping Martinez lead dazed, trembling Smith out of the aisle and toward the far stairs to the stage.

He stood near the doors, but not in range to be hit by them. The muted lively crowd noises behind him interfered with his ability to hear conversations from the stage. Balton led his group of board members to the chairs, where Gray and Martinez had already ensconced themselves with Smith.

Aldenrud, Balton, and Costigan had their heads together, looking down at something on her tablet.

Perry and the other guard swore loudly when they realized the first booth door wouldn't stay closed. They jiggled the lever and pushed with their hips, but as soon as they let go, the door swung open.

Balton strode over. Arvik hid a smile, knowing that to Balton, all magical problems looked like a nail. Sure enough, his hammer of a spell blew the door off its hinges. As a bonus, the doors of the next two booths popped open as well.

"Magister Balton," said Costigan, "please go sit with the

sales clerks. They may need your assistance if a buyer causes trouble." Her tone brooked no argument. In the auction space, she ruled with ruthless efficiency. "We'll use three booths. Perry, McReady, Foster, you'll be at the booths. Magister Díaz will let the buyers in and seal the doors, then come up here to keep the shifters quiet. We'll skip the hands-on inspection period of the merchandise. Buyer pays first, then we hand over the prize." She smiled briefly. "We'll throw in the shackles as a free bonus."

She said something off-mic to Aldenrud. He replied and pointed toward the back doors. She shook her head and said something else, pointing to the board members. He frowned and stalked over to stand with them.

By Arvik's count, everyone was in the auction area. The remaining two cashiers sat at their desks in the far corner, near the stairs. If nothing else had, the skeleton staffing would have told him the owners had decided the business was a lost cause.

"Magister Díaz, open the doors, please."

As he did so, her warm, professional voice boomed in the buyers' lobby, inviting them in for the most exclusive sale the auction house had ever offered.

He hid his impatience as the thirty buyers sauntered in, some laughing, some holding drinks, all holding numbered bidder cards. A few gave him casual glances, and one gave him an empty champagne glass. Active wizard magic, mostly illusions and enhancers, pushed at his senses.

As soon as the guard cleared the threshold, Arvik shut the doors and tripped the charmed locks, which armed the rest of the defenses. The lobby and the stairs to the surface helipad featured a dozen painful-to-lethal failsafes designed to keep captives—and non-paying buyers—from getting away.

He walked briskly to the stairs and up onto the stage,

behind the row of empty display booths, to where the shifters sat in semi-darkness.

Costigan queued music and announced the rules and procedures for the auctions.

Arvik slowed as if unable to see well, giving him the chance to check Rayne as he passed. Jealousy stung when he saw she was holding Lerro's hand. It eased slightly when he realized she was casting a lower-level version of the healing spell he'd used on her twenty minutes ago. He sourly hoped Lerro wasn't enjoying it.

The first up for auction was Mondo, the berserker gorilla with the scars of a cage fighter. He sold for Costigan's opening price, to one of the Imperium infiltrators.

Arvik stood a couple of meters in front of the stage doors, dividing his attention between the restive shifters and a series of spells he was knitting together on the spot. The Shifter Tribunal operatives, including Rayne, would never believe the wizards were buying the shifters to get them out of harm's way. He hoped his new plan worked.

After two more slow sales, a bidding war started for the fourth captive, a crocodile shifter.

Unexpectedly, Aldenrud appeared from behind a darkened booth, headed straight for Arvik. At the last second, he veered around and opened one of the doors. "Be right back."

The faint odor of sour fear hit Arvik's nose as the door closed. He remembered Aldenrud's record was littered with lucky breaks.

Arvik's instincts said time just ran out. He touched his earring to activate the spell series and send the signal to his people.

Arvik-as-Arturo ambled to the end of the shifter line

and around it, headed for a look at who'd just won the bidding war.

As he passed Rayne and Lerro, he whispered just for their sensitive shifter ears. "The power of three. Stairs at the end of A Wing. I made a tunnel. Run human, and don't touch the walls. Endgame starts now."

6

———

Ever since Rayne realized what Díaz was doing for the shifters as he walked down the line, she'd been surreptitiously scheming with Lerro how to take advantage of the gift and communicating the plan to their fellow captives. Thank the moon goddess the guards weren't paying any attention to them and Díaz was on their side.

Lerro wasn't trembling any more, but he'd been beaten and starved for the last year, and the knockout spell hadn't helped. She used a little healing spell to share her energy. If they managed to liberate the shifters, she planned to ask him what the "karma" deal had been about, but not today.

They'd rejected the hidden fairy portal as the way out. She could operate portals, but couldn't change the destination. The other end could be a leap into fire instead of freedom. And the hidden emergency exit in the former shifter wing was underwater.

They'd have to go for the stairs at the end of the intake branch of the administration wing. The staff and contractor hunters preferred the elevators, but the secured and spell-protected stairway led to the same camouflage-covered parking lot and a narrow dirt road that connected to a winding paved road.

Just the thought of being outside again set her inner wolf to baying. Like most shifters, she didn't do well in underground cages. Everyone had coping mechanisms. Hers was to focus on her mission objectives and dream of the full moon on a silent, snowy landscape.

She told Lerro what she'd noticed in her two recent trips to the admin wing. They agreed they could ignore the cameras, but not the broad-spectrum life-sign suppression spells. None of the shifters had the charmed staff badges that would let them come and go. Information she'd elicited from previous cellmates said the spells wouldn't kill; they'd just knock any magical species cold, even humans with shifter-mate potential.

As much as she wished she had the magical power of her sister or Díaz, she didn't, so she'd have to deal with the spells once they got closer.

The auction out front got louder as a bidding war started for the crocodile shifter. Lerro used it for cover to tell Olivia, the capybara shifter next to him, to get ready to run and to pass it on. He mimed tapping his shackles together three times.

Rayne was watching the progress of the message when Díaz walked slowly around her, whispering his own message about the endgame.

Adrenaline rushed through her. Díaz's rising magic made her want to writhe in pleasure. She'd deal with that later. He was headed toward the front of the stage.

She tapped her wrists together three times and caught the shackles. She did the same with her ankle restraints, leaving them half on so they'd fool a casual glance.

The winning bidder number was announced with a fanfare of music. The audience applauded.

Lerro mimicked her actions. Like a chain reaction, the movements spread up the line. Fortunately, the guards were busy leading the crocodile shifter out of the booth and setting up the next one.

Magic exploded from the direction of the audience, buffeting her senses. The temperature dropped twenty degrees. Icy-cold howling winds and blowing snowflakes followed.

Endgame, indeed.

She leaped to her feet. "Exit! Stay human!" She urged Lerro toward the doors, knowing the shifters would follow. Lerro was a legend.

The shifter closest to the guard Perry head-punched her unconscious before she could twitch. McReady reached for his gun, then crumpled from a blow to the head from a swinging shackle.

Rayne used the technique she'd learned from watching Díaz to unlock and open wide the double doors in front of Lerro. He shouted and ran out. The captives swarmed after him.

She could feel where Díaz was without seeing him. His magic pulled at her senses.

Alarms sounded. Bright lights in the ceiling strobed.

The winds picked up, making it harder to get to Foster, the third guard, who was on his knees.

She shoved Ndelo, the hyena shifter, away from him, toward the door. "Go! He's mine!" She snarled possessively, allowing some of her true dire wolf to show.

Ndelo's eyes went wide with fear as he stumbled away, then ran after the other shifters.

Foster, blinded by blood and pain, took a wild swing at her.

She evaded, then put him in a controlling headlock. "It's

me. I've got you. Shift!" She added alpha power to her order. "Now!"

His body obeyed her command faster than he'd have been able to do it on his own. His guard uniform shredded. She held on to him until she was sure he'd found his lean red wolf.

She picked up two of his weapons and gave him a final hug. "Go find your aunt." His nose would lead him to the woman called Gray, even if her board member glamour fooled his wolf's eyes in the terrible winds of battle.

Foster had gone undercover before she had. She owed him her life several times over.

A hammer of an attack spell split her head wide open with pain. Her own magic made her more vulnerable than most shifters to such spells.

She shook it off as she fought the wind and snow to make her way to where Díaz's life energy burned bright. She couldn't go after her primary objective until she knew he was safe.

Or as safe as he could be, in a magical war zone.

Arvik's Arctic-winter spell was burning through his magical power reserves, but he couldn't stop now. The captives needed time to escape, buyers outnumbered the Imperium agents two to one, and Balton was cornered and dangerous.

Two running witches frantically threw spells at the lobby doors. The guard crumpled. Arvik sent a gust of wind to knock them back into the arms of the pursuing Imperium agents.

Across the stage, Balton and Costigan stood with their backs to the wall, surrounded by four Imperium wizards.

Balton unleashed a tremendous power bolt. Two Imperium wizards fell back, stunned. Costigan slumped to the floor.

Balton pushed off from the wall toward the back exit. His shield protected him from the force of Arvik's wind, but not from kinetic force of the leaping Bengal tiger that bowled him over sideways.

Below Arvik in the audience, three disguised buyers huddled together, working on a spell. Fairies, he concluded from the fact that he could only feel the shape of their magic, not the substance. He sent more wind to overwhelm their words, but he wasn't sure it helped.

The sensation of summer sun warmed his back. He didn't need to look to know it came from Rayne. His inner animals leaned in toward the light.

He glanced at her as she stepped up beside him. "You should be running."

"Says the man about to be taken on a fairy-ring thrill ride." She pointed and triggered the lightning rod in her hand at a white-haired man. He jolted back into the others. Their illusions blinked out, revealing long-limbed blue mountain fairies. Plasma danced over them all as they slumped in a daze.

"Thanks. I can't see fairy magic." He usually didn't admit his weaknesses, but he felt he could trust her.

Balton release another power bolt, sending the tiger flying. A large red wolf bit into his meaty calf. Balton screamed in pain and swung a fist at the wolf's head. The scarred gorilla named Mondo blocked the punch, then pulled the wolf out of reach. Two Imperium wizards stepped in to shoot Balton with a charmed web.

The web expanded to cover struggling Balton, then glowed bright pink and made him disappear with an ear-popping air rush. The Imperium's holding dungeon just got a new customer.

With the Imperium and Tribunal teams finally working together, the buyers knew they were losing. Several of them just sat down and held up their hands in surrender.

Beside him, Rayne shivered and put her arms across her chest.

He pulled back on his magic. With no more power, the Arctic winds would soon die on their own. "Want to go someplace quieter? Like, say, the cash room where they keep the backup sales records? Maybe check to be sure that no shifter got left behind?"

She laughed. "Best pick-up line I've heard in a year." She gestured toward the back exit with a graceful flourish. "Lead on."

He headed toward the exit, giving her a smart-ass smile instead of the kiss he'd been fantasizing about. Best not to start something he couldn't finish. She might want to kiss him, too, but he doubted she'd consent to mate with a monster.

7

Rayne opened the third file drawer. This one contained folders marked with employee names. She wanted them all, but she pulled the ones for Aldenrud, Balton, Díaz, Costigan, Foster, and a handful of others.

The room-sized vault stank of acidic sweat. Someone, and her guess was Aldenrud, had cleaned out most of the actual cash. A few bills littered the floor, suggesting haste.

Díaz swore in Spanish and pointed to empty shelves in the tall cabinet he'd just opened. "Backups are gone."

"If I were skimming, I wouldn't leave a backtrail, either." She closed the file drawer and opened the bottom one. Instead of files, it had a lid with a combination. "Bring your criminally good lock-pick spell over here and open this."

She picked up the files and the confiscated lightning rod, then stepped back to give him room. She hugged the files to her chest to hide her hard nipples and to keep from putting her hands on him like she wanted. Simple skin-to-skin contact sent her hormones singing. If they ever made love, she'd probably spontaneously combust.

While he knelt, she quickly shifted to her wolf with its

maned-wolf illusion, then back into human, without the files and weapon, and with better clothes. After six weeks of wearing nothing but flimsy flats or going barefoot on filthy concrete floors, sturdy boots had never felt so good. If only her trick worked with food.

He stood and crossed his arms. "Impressive talent."

"Thanks." Her wolf urged her to tell him all about it and find out all about him, but dire wolves didn't understand about time and place, or bells that couldn't be unrung. Not all true mates were destined to be together.

She glanced down at the opened lid and frowned. "Why leave all this cash?" She leaned closer, but a frisson of magic had her backing up. "Illusion trap. We just triggered something."

At the other end of the room, the heavy vault door was swinging shut.

Díaz leaped over the counting table and grabbed the handle. The door slowed but didn't stop.

Borrowing strength and speed from her wolf, she pushed the table into the opening. It delayed the door long enough for them both to scramble over it and out into the hallway. The table bent and broke as the vault door inexorably closed and locked.

She grinned at him. "That was a blast. Want to see if Aldenrud's office measures up?"

His answering grin lit up his face. The surly wizard persona hid a sinfully enticing man. "Maybe for a second date." He pointed down the hall. "We should get back before we're missed."

That sobered her. Real life was never as much fun as it was cracked up to be.

They trotted together back to the main admin hall and the ruined hub. As they approached the auction wing, the straw-in-a-tornado feel of wild magic scraped her senses.

Battlefield magic took days to dissipate in the open air. Who knew how long it would take in an underground facility?

As they slowed to walk through the doors to the auction stage, she fought a strong impulse to grab Díaz's hand and never let go. Inner wolves lived for the moment, so it was up to the human side to consider consequences and make the tough choices. She forced herself to politely nod to him once, then cross left to the Tribunal team.

Gray, whose real name was Celia Wong, stood with her nephew Donovan, formerly known as the guard Foster. Nearby, the gorilla shifter called Mondo stood, arms crossed, looking grumpy. He sported a couple of fading bruises on his thighs, a puffy eye, and a healing split lip. The capybara shifter and the crocodile shifter sat on the floor looking exhausted. None of them wore clothes. Rayne felt over-dressed.

She looked around for familiar faces and scents. "Where are the others?"

Celia put her hands on her hips. "Mr. Brooker canceled our strike team." From her tone, she didn't agree.

Rayne nodded, glad her boss had decided to let the Imperium team handle the fight and the aftermath. Too easy to incur friendly-fire casualties if you don't know who your friends are.

Celia waved toward a circular ring of dust on the wall. "Brooker and Myelle ordered the medical emergency portal and took Lingram with them. Kilisha is investigating the real portal in the boardroom." She cast a dark glance toward the four remaining Wizard Imperium agents on the other side of the stage, where Díaz stood with them. "The wizards created their own portal and took the staff and the buyers." The Shifter Tribunal usually contracted with fairies for creating portals.

Rayne wondered if the Imperium would share the intelligence they gained from their prisoners. The Tribunal had a right to know, since shifter victims had outnumbered the other races by ten to one, but the exchange would probably take months to negotiate.

Celia's frown deepened. "Who was that feral shifter who attacked Lingram? We'll want him for questioning. And the enemy wizard who you claim helped you."

Rayne's temper spiked. "Lingram shot first. That shifter and that wizard saved my life. The wizard freed the captives and cleared the way out."

Donovan cleared his throat. "Díaz did save her life. The shifter-wing guards nearly beat her to death." A haunted expression crossed his face. They'd planned the risky maneuver together, but he'd had to pretend he liked watching a shifter get hurt.

Rayne wanted to hug him. Undercover work sometimes required making terrible choices for a successful mission. Only another field agent could understand.

Celia's face twisted in a sour frown. "How very convenient for a slave market run by wizards to be 'cleaned up' by wizards."

Rayne thinned her lips. "How very convenient for the Tribunal to deny auction house rumors for *four years* without investigating."

Celia's jaw tightened and her eyes went cold. "The Tribunal thanks you for your service. We'll take it from here." She exerted alpha dominance to quell Rayne's attitude.

Rayne let it roll on by. Ice Age dire wolves did not take orders from modern alphas, regardless of species.

Celia frowned, just like every alpha who had ever tried to get Rayne to submit. Her nostrils wrinkled. "You need a shower."

Behind her, Donovan rolled his eyes. "Chill. She's on our side."

Celia had the grace to look abashed. "Myelle is coming back with the main portal in a few minutes."

Rayne turned and walked away before she said something else she'd have to apologize for later. Politicians and alphas made her crazy, and Celia was both in spades. They'd recruited and trained her for the "executive board" operation because no one would doubt her in that role.

Rayne's sly inner wolf and her willful feet wanted to take her closer to Díaz, who was talking to the wizards and pointing toward the closed lobby doors. She compromised by detouring to the auctioneer's station. Costigan had been a cold, money-motivated asshole, but she'd been highly skilled at her job.

The array of controls made the podium look like a jumbo jet's flight deck. The top half featured buttons marked for audience and stage lighting, lobby lights, sound, multiple microphones, and eight computer micro-ports. The bottom buttons and sliders apparently controlled the display booths and the security measures that included magic melded with technology. Skyla, magic prodigy and already almost a magister, would have loved taking it apart.

Rayne sent a prayer to the moon goddess for the safety and health of her beloved sister, who she'd treated abominably by faking her own death, even cutting her off from the family tracking spell to make it convincing. For that, she would owe penance for as long as she lived.

Agents weren't supposed to cry. She knelt to check deep into the shelves below. Her questing fingers found and latched onto a familiar shape.

A chill went through her. It was the tablet computer that Costigan had rarely been without. Strong instinct said to take it and hide it. Her gift for finding hidden things bonged in her chest like she'd hit a casino jackpot.

She'd bet the house that it had the sales records she was looking for. Maybe even a clue as to the true owners of the auction operation for Díaz.

She reluctantly let it go and stood up again, pretending to study the more cryptically marked controls.

The sad truth was, she couldn't share her find with the Tribunal team until she first imaged its contents. She'd lost the stars in her eyes as to the righteousness of the Tribunal some time ago. Lingram's rogue, unwarranted attack on Díaz had just been the latest evidence.

Besides, the Tribunal wouldn't share it with the Imperium in time to do any good, and she owed Díaz the chance to achieve his objective.

And if the Tribunal figured out why she wanted the names from the records, they'd put her under house arrest for the next decade.

The equally sad truth was that she currently only trusted four people. Her sister, her boss, and Lerro weren't around, so that left Díaz, or whatever his real name was. Hell, she wouldn't have been using her real name if the hunters hadn't caught her off guard and confiscated her personal wallet. Not her finest day.

A distant-but-getting-closer yell had all the shifters turning to look toward the back entrance.

"Ru-u-u-n! Hel-l-l-fr-o-o-g!" Kilisha's voice.

"Fuck!" Donovan lunged toward the two seated shifters and urged them to stand. "She must have opened the boardroom portal without the charm." He pointed to the small side door that led to the cashiers' office. "Close the door, then hit the red panic button. Mondo, you're the strongest. Go with them. Protect them."

Rayne shouted to the wizards. "Shield or portal out, now. Hellfrog coming."

Kilisha's yelling changed from a human yell to an eagle's screech. Subsonic growling accompanied the sound of claws scraping on concrete.

"What's a hellfrog?" asked one of the wizards.

"Big elven frog-thing with teeth and claws," said the one next to him.

"Shut up and shield!" said another.

Donovan was shifting into his red wolf form. His aunt Celia was already on four feet, finishing her shift into a large gray wolf.

Rayne ran to the doors to close one side and threw its bolts. Wizard magic flared behind her, but not from Díaz, so it felt like sandpaper.

She grabbed the other door, ready to slam it. "Kilisha! This way!"

Moments later, a charcoal-gray African martial eagle flew sideways through the single door, wingtips scraping the doorjamb as she flapped up toward the ceiling.

Rayne slammed the door closed, but it fought her, wanting to open. She braced her back against it. "Díaz! Door!" His spell to free the rest of the shifters was coming back to bite them.

The flare of his magic came too late to stop the hurtling hellfrog from ramming the door open and skidding onto the stage.

Rayne shifted as she flew through the air. She regained her footing on four feet and got her first look at the enemy.

The shiny green-and-black-spotted creature stood four feet tall and looked like a cross between a poisonous toad and a fat beetle. It had a lizard's running legs with taloned toes, orbital eyes, and a huge wide mouth full of crooked alligator teeth. The red-lipped mouth drooled.

Unless re-leashed or stopped, hellfrogs relentlessly pursue their designated quarry. She suspected in this case, the quarry was anyone in the facility.

The hellfrog ignored her and the two growling wolves to its left and zeroed in on the five humans to the right, with Díaz in front.

It launched itself toward them, only to bounce off the reinforced wizard shield.

The impact pushed all the wizards backward. One fell off the stage and landed on her ass, three feet below. She scrambled back onto the stage.

The hellfrog opened its jaws impossibly wide and tried to bite Díaz but couldn't get a grip on the shield wall. Hellfrogs were stubborn, but not bright. The wizards argued among themselves about spells to use.

To the left, the cashiers' office door made a heavy thunking sound, signaling the dragon-proof defenses had activated.

Donovan's red wolf and Celia's gray wolf snarled at the hellfrog.

It swiveled one eye toward them, but went back to trying to get at the wizards, this time by digging at the base of the shield near Díaz's feet.

Rayne growled at the hellfrog threatening her mate. Under her maned-wolf illusion, she was one pissed-off dire wolf. *Mine!*

The hellfrog swung its massive head toward her, then turned to face her.

No spell she knew would kill a nearly indestructible hellfrog, but the explosives in the fairy wing might slow it down long enough for the rest of them to portal out.

She barked a challenge, then spun to race out the back doors.

The now *closed* back doors. Damnit!

She twisted her back haunches away from the hellfrog's leap and bite. Her thick fur and wooly undercoat meant she only got a stinging scrape.

Stalking to her right, she put the full threat of her dire wolf into her growl. Modern mammals atavistically feared the sound of an Ice Age dire wolf on the hunt. She hoped it worked on amphibians.

The hellfrog froze.

Then magic flared, and its eyes glowed brighter red. It scuttled toward her, all teeth.

She danced away again, then slashed a tearing bite on its fat haunch, drawing blood.

It screamed in pain, but the wound was already closing.

A weird metallic taste on her tongue sent a magical shockwave through her system.

"Don't swallow the blood!" Díaz's warning penetrated her adrenalin-fueled tunnel focus.

She shook her head to get the tainted saliva out of her mouth. Her maned-wolf illusion flickered. She let it go, rather than take time and energy to restore it.

She feigned an attack to the left, then leaped high and over to the right. She pushed off a darkened display booth to slam her wide shoulders into its side.

The hellfrog slid twenty feet. Its legs tangled in the pile of chains and shackles on the floor.

Díaz's warm magic flared. The chains snaked around the hellfrog's body, and multiple sets of shackles clamped around its legs and torso.

The hellfrog's eyes and mouth glowed red. The chains and shackles glowed electric blue, sending jolting shocks through the hellfrog's body. The dark elven magic that powered the hellfrog clashed with the auction house's wizard magic in the ethereal plane, grating on her nerves.

Fairy magic bloomed behind her.

She shifted to human and ran toward the opening portal. "Myelle! We have a hellfrog!"

She glanced to the right. Díaz crouched on the stage, concentrating on the hellfrog. The rest of the wizards crowded together in the audience section below. The sandpaper of their shield magic faded, replaced by the dust-storm feel of wizard portal magic.

Celia began shifting to human. Donovan did the same.

Rayne moved closer to Díaz, ready to protect him since he no longer had a shield. Only his magic on the auction-house shackles was keeping everyone safe from the struggling hellfrog. She should have thought to bring weapons when she shifted back to human.

The fairy portal stabilized. Rayne spared a quick look to see Myelle striding through in human form, carrying a big elven-tech gun, accompanied by two human-shaped and four tiger-shaped guards, all in armor.

Donovan rushed over and hurriedly told them about the shifters in the cashiers' office.

Kilisha, still in eagle form, flew through the portal and vanished.

The hellfrog glowed red all over. More blue-glowing shackles latched onto its limbs.

With an audible snap, the wizard portal near the auditorium seats stabilized. The pink-haired female wizard stepped through and vanished.

The black-haired wizard ran to the stage. "Díaz! We can't keep the portal for long. The room's defenses are fighting us! Grab the dire wolf and let's go!"

Díaz's eyes flashed gold. "She's not a prize, Sutaraman."

The man looked frustrated. "Port now. Argue later."

Celia's voice barking orders grabbed Rayne's attention.

"Arrest that wizard and Chekal. He works for the auction house and has her under his spell. Careful. She's an unregistered mythic." The accusatory tone was unmistakable.

Celia pushed one of the human-shaped guards toward Rayne.

The guard looked to Myelle, who shook her head in irritation and pointed toward the portal. "Escort Counselor Wong to the medic. She's obviously suffering from head trauma."

The guard unceremoniously threw protesting Celia over her shoulder and trotted through the portal and vanished.

The trembling hellfrog took one slow step toward the fairy portal, dragging the chains and shackles with it.

Myelle turned to watch Donovan and the tiger guard leading Mondo in gorilla form and the other former captives up the stairs to the stage and toward the portal.

The black-haired wizard still argued with Díaz. "...don't want to share. Fuck you. Find your own way back!" The wizard stormed toward the portal, where only one other wizard remained. Within seconds, they both vanished. The wizard portal snapped closed.

The hellfrog sent out a scream loud enough to shatter glass.

Every shifter in the room winced in pain. The hellfrog's threat lit a fire under their feet as they sped toward the fairy portal. One armored tiger stayed with Myelle.

Fear tried to crawl through Rayne's ears and into her brain, but her inner dire wolf was having none of it. She used the alpha's trick of half-shifting and howled like she'd found easy dinner.

The hellfrog quieted but continued inching toward the open fairy portal.

Myelle beckoned. "Let's go. Bring the wizard as your guest."

Rayne glanced at Díaz's gargoyle-like demeanor. Hoping

her intuition wasn't about to make them hellfrog victims, she shook her head. "Nah, I'm good. I'll find my own way home."

Myelle hesitated, searching Rayne's expression.

After a longer moment, Myelle turned and strode through the portal. After the tip of the tiger's tale vanished, the portal winked out with a pop of air displacement.

The red-glowing hellfrog slowly turned toward her and Díaz, dragging the weight of the blue-glowing shackles and chains.

"So, Magister Díaz," she said brightly, "how long do we have before the auction house's magic fails?"

8

Arvik's head pounded from the effort to channel magic into the shackles. "We have five minutes, maybe. I'm running out of steam." Disparate thoughts splintered his focus. The wizard strike team needed purging. His inner animals wanted at the hellfrog. Rayne's true dire-wolf form kicked ass. He vowed to be worthy of the trust she'd honored him with.

She pointed toward the doors. "The fairy wing is lined with explosives. Could we lure it there?" Her talent for discovering things kicked ass, too.

"No. I destroyed the trigger mechanism last night when Balton was distracted." Back when he'd imagined he knew what was about to go down.

She smiled knowingly as she crossed to the auctioneer's podium. "Best-laid plans."

Nice that he didn't have to explain or apologize. "If I can free up my magic, I can emergency-port us out of the facility."

She crouched to reach into the bottom shelves. "Then let's go while we can." A smile flitted across her face.

"Bingo." She stood, clutching to her chest a glittery-gold rectangle that he recognized as Costigan's tablet. "Which exit?"

"Back doors. The front entrance is too well protected. I need distance from our new *amigo*." He tilted his head toward the straining hellfrog.

The laden amphibian took another slow step toward him.

She nodded, then tilted her head toward the doors. "Are they unlocked?"

He flicked a spare bit of magic toward them. "They are now." Both doors swung open.

She darted glances around the space with a calculating look. "Will the chains hold without your help?"

"Not long. They weren't designed to work together."

She nodded. "Then you need to be closer to the door so we can run."

Before he could reply, she shifted into her magnificent dire-wolf form. Thick white fur covered an enormous wolf with wide jaws and wider shoulders, and brilliant orange-red eyes. Her head was almost the height of his human shoulders, and he was close to two meters tall. He'd been freakishly tall among his people, centuries ago. She made him feel almost short.

She circled behind him to turn and face the hellfrog. The threat growl she gave sent a shiver up his human spine, but not of fear. He hadn't felt a pack connection like that in centuries.

The hellfrog swung its head toward her and screamed back. More importantly, it took one step toward her, then another.

She bared her lethal teeth and growled again, calling it the canine equivalent of a dung-eating leg-humper. The hellfrog took two more dragging steps.

Arvik eased right, gathering more stray magic to channel to the chains while calculating his route to the doors. For once, his inner animals gave him their cunning without arguing about eating nasty amphibians or protecting their mate.

One of the dragging chains began melting. The drips of slag charred the wood floor beneath it.

"Time!" he shouted.

Rayne sidestepped farther left, luring the hellfrog with her.

Borrowing speed from his animals, he ran around the white-hot mass of chains and through the open doors. He turned just as Rayne's white wolf vaulted through the opening and landed behind him, scrabbling for purchase on the hard floor.

Hastily pulling stored magic from his silver necklace, he slammed the doors shut and activated the auction room's defenses, cutting off a rising scream from the hellfrog.

He pivoted and started running across the hub to the admin wing. "Clinic!"

She bounded ahead and beat him to the door, then shifted to human in seconds. He envied her speed.

He opened the clinic door with his palmprint and magic. She followed him inside and watched while he sealed it.

He rolled up his shirtsleeves, revealing his wristbands. "These have an emergency exit portal spell. Where to?" he asked.

"What are the choices?"

"Anywhere one of us has been and can picture in our mind." He frowned. "Your people want me for interrogation, and my soon-to-be-ex colleagues want you, probably for less noble purposes. I vote someplace neutral and defensible."

Her mouth twisted in thought. "Ever heard of Kotoyeesinay?"

"The Wyoming sanctuary town?" He nodded. "Yes, but they may not want me."

"My family has a long-standing reservation. I can vouch for you as a temporary guest." She caught his eye. "Anything I should know about that will make them bring pitchforks instead of the welcome wagon?"

He shook his head. "It's… complicated."

A storm of wild, chaotic magic blew through the ethereal plane. The chain and shackle magic had failed. From her uneasy expression, she, too, had felt the magic blowout.

He held out his hands to her. "Let's visit Kotoyeesinay."

She ignored his hands and stepped in to embrace him instead. "I'll picture the town's border. You send us there."

Her body against his threatened to shatter coherent thought. The unmistakable scent of her arousal sent heat arrowing to his groin, hardening him. His animals leaped forward, reaching for her dire wolf.

He couldn't let any of that happen before he told her who he was. What he was. He hastily slammed his wristbands together behind her shoulders and triggered the stored portal spell.

Physical and ethereal winds deafened him and stole his breath. He wrapped himself around Rayne, afraid of losing her.

A holographic image floated into view—a high mountain road surrounded by evergreens and a town in the distance. Lights strobed from beach white to space black. Deep Arctic cold flushed through him, draining his magic fast. The only warmth came from the woman in his arms. Gravity sucked them into a vortex, then dropped them into freefall.

The mountain scene gained weight and substance, like a ground rush after parachuting out of a plane. Twilight made long shadows of trees. He used his waning magic to envelop himself and Rayne in his shield to protect them from the inevitable tumble on the asphalt road.

The air swatted them sideways.

He desperately held on to Rayne and his shield.

They somersaulted through the air and ricocheted off a rock wall into a bank of snow.

Rayne cried out.

Agony lanced through his left leg.

His magic sputtered out. Cold settled into his bones, dulling the pain.

Silence and darkness, then nothing.

"Díaz!"

The urgency in Rayne's voice made him open his eyes. He lay on his back in cold, wet snow, looking at the night sky. Had it been this dark before?

The silhouette of her beautiful face blocked his view of the twinkling stars. "Your calf is impaled on a deadfall branch. I can free you, but after that, I don't have enough magic right now to power a healing spell, and I don't think you do, either. You'll have to shift to one of your other forms."

It should have worried him that she'd discovered he was a shifter, especially one with two animal souls, but he couldn't remember why. "Where are we?"

"One mountain to the north of Kotoyeesinay. I think your shield bounced off their shield." Worry seeped into her tone. "You need to shift."

Before he could tell her he couldn't, his inner animals

outvoted him and commandeered his voice. "Break the gold chain on my neck and wrap it around my wrists."

She yanked the chain hard, tearing into his skin, drawing a hiss from him.

"I'll kiss it and make it better later." Grabbing his hands, she bound his wrists together with the chain.

At the insistence of his animals, he whispered the key.

The self-imposed spell cracked open and fell away, leaving him feeling light as a feather, and truly alive. Cold melted away.

He'd been chained so long he'd forgotten how it felt to be free. His sharpened senses took in the detailed shape of the gnarled tree, the sound of Rayne's rapid breathing, and the scent of blood. His blood.

Beside him, Rayne gasped and shivered. "That is some spell. Now can you shift?"

He nodded. "Let me see the damage."

She helped him sit, then pulled a heavy-duty flashlight out of her winter jacket pocket and shined the bright light on his leg. He made a mental note to ask her about her astonishing ability to materialize clothes and other things.

The offending branch pierced his calf through and through. Torn leather from his pants infiltrated the wound at the entry point. Nasty. He could feel his innate magic working on the cracked bone. He'd have to re-break the bone later if it healed crooked, or he'd be permanently maimed. True shifters didn't have that problem.

She pointed to the tree trunk. "I took advantage of your nap to roll you and it over so I could free your leg." She blew out a quick breath. "I can cut your clothes off and cast a painkiller spell, but it's still going to hurt like a stinkin' son of a bitch."

"I can take care of my clothes. Save the spell for later. I can't shift if I'm numb."

She nodded. "Okay. Sorry in advance."

With quick, ruthless efficiency, she pulled him off the branch. He yelled as pain exploded in his leg.

Her human eyes glowed dire-wolf orange. "Shift."

Steely alpha commands usually had little effect on him, but his inner wolf used it to overpower his human reticence. He barely had time to siphon the shift magic to save his clothes.

Thirty seconds later, he stood in oversized timber wolf form. The renewal magic took care of his aches and pains, and remade his leg bones.

It was the first time he'd stood on four paws in close to a year. He shook all over, loose fur flying, just because he could.

The smells had his nose working overtime, taking in everything. Rayne's ever-changing scent fascinated him, along with everything else about her. He took several steps closer to her.

She crouched and held out her hand to him. "Impressive. Let me see your leg."

Arvik-the-wild-wolf dove toward her feet in a barrel roll, exposing his belly.

Laughing, she ran her hand over his back leg, plunging her fingers into his fur. "I see this beast of yours is as shameless as mine."

She slid her hand up toward his head to scratch behind his ear. "It'll be easier to find the town in wolf form, but we'll have to shift back once we get to the border, so we can ring the doorbell." Her tone sounded practical, but his superb ears detected threads of sadness and regret.

He wanted to talk to her, find out what was wrong, and hold her until she felt better, but that was just selfishness. Considering their careers and the current troubles with their respective employers, neither of them would be free to consider a relationship anytime soon, much less a mating. And that was child's play compared to the likely insurmountable problem of his heritage.

He respected Rayne too much to let her get involved with someone both shifter clans and the First Peoples tribes of the north considered a supernatural enemy.

He rolled to his feet and shook his fur again. Talking could wait. He wasn't going to pass up what might be his only chance to run with his mate through the snow on a moonlit night.

9

Rayne shifted to her dire wolf, glad for the chance to heal the painful bruises she'd suffered from their freefall into a mountainside. She decided against restoring her maned wolf illusion until after she had food. Dire wolves could go days without eating, but it tended to make them consider people as potential appetizers instead of potential allies.

The constant wind ruffled her outer fur but couldn't touch her thick undercoat. She was built for much colder climates than mid-autumn snow in the Rocky Mountains of Wyoming.

Díaz's noble timber wolf looked proud and untamable. Gray and white fur, wide head, brilliantly intelligent gold eyes. Almost as big as she was, and he smelled intriguingly, divinely complex, of wolf, fresh snow, and sea salt. The darker animal in him, hidden well below the surface, felt almost alien, though she couldn't say why she thought so. She knew practically nothing about him. Hell, she didn't even know his real name. Not that it mattered. As an older shifter and a field agent, he probably had dozens.

She made herself ignore the compelling mystery of the shifter who could be her mate and pointed her nose downhill.

Over open tundra, wolves ran far and fast. Picking their way down an unfamiliar mountainside in the weak moonlight took considerably more time. Even so, the open air and freedom to be a wolf again made it worthwhile. Running with a pack mate made it perfect, though her stubborn human side warned her not to get used to it.

Three hours later found them approaching the Kotoyeesinay border, marked by a winding two-lane road illuminated by a single, dim pole light. The invisible shield felt almost electrified, with a phantom smell of ozone. Díaz sat and shifted into human form, wearing his thin gray silk shirt, torn leather pants, and heavy work boots. Even tired and disheveled, he was a devilishly handsome human.

She considered her inventory of clothes, then shifted into hiking shoes, flannel-lined jeans, a turtleneck, and a hooded winter parka. This time, she remembered to bring a heavy-duty charmed knife along with the flashlight.

She hid a frown as she walked with Díaz down the slope to the road. He still favoring his left leg.

It had been a mistake to throw herself into his arms for the emergency portal jump, because now, she couldn't forget how perfectly the hard planes of his body aligned with hers. His magic revved her engines, leaving her with a constant flush of desire. And worries about him being hurt or cold stole her focus from planning how to get into Kotoyeesinay, report to her boss, then crash and burn. Well, eat first, *then* crash and burn.

She caught up with him at the edge of the asphalt. "The border wasn't this tight the last time I was here, but that was thirty years ago."

Three more steps, and the barrier became a visible shimmer of magical power.

"Stay," he said, not looking at her as he barred her way with his arm. "I'll test it."

Exasperation ran through her. "Son of an alpha." She muttered it like the curse it was.

He dropped his arm and turned to look at her. "What?"

And this was the cave-dweller that her inner wolf wanted to mate. "This isn't obedience school."

From the look on his face, he was replaying his actions in his mind. He opened his mouth to speak, then hesitated and closed it. His expression closed with it. "Try going in without me." A thread of bleakness laced his tone.

"Not happening." She didn't need her wolf's urging to reject his suggestion. She owed him her life three times over, even if he was thick-skulled. "If they won't let us both in, we can walk to the next town." She pointed a thumb in the direction of the mountains behind them. "Roads always lead somewhere."

He snorted. "To hell, usually."

"Been there, got the stinky T-shirt and sweatpants." A memory from years before surfaced. "I think it's a matter of asking."

She crossed the road and touched fingers to the lamppost. "I am Rayne Chekal, wolf shifter. I hereby ask for sanctuary for me and guest status for my companion, a wizard called Díaz."

After long seconds, a mid-range voice seemed to emanate from everywhere. "One moment."

Flashy sorcery flared, bathing her in the soothing comfort of a cozy home. Underneath, a subtler elven spell probed at her secrets, but she fended it off. They could damn well ask her in person instead of being sneaky about it.

Díaz's face was back to stony, but his shield tickled her like a caress before it subsided.

"Provisional sanctuary granted for you both," said the voice. "Please proceed to the sheriff's station. Do you need assistance or medical attention?"

The border barrier raised an archway over the road. An image of a map formed in the air, with a route marked to the sheriff's station.

She caught Díaz's eye. "In, or the open road?"

Surprise flitted across his face. "In." His mouth twitched. "They have cookies."

She laughed, delighted at the reappearance of his humor. "And steaks."

She touched the lamppost again. "Could we get a ride into town? Díaz had a disagreement with a tree."

The voice replied after a long moment. "Yes. Look for the magic carpet."

The well-lit lobby of the Kotoyeesinay sheriff station looked well designed and surprisingly inviting, but sadly, offered no cookies, much less steaks. The big railroad-style clock said it was a few minutes before five. Rayne was too tired to guess how long until dawn.

At the long, standing-height desk, a uniformed deputy handed Rayne a tablet that displayed a brief form. "Sorry, we're down to one working tablet right now, so give it to him when you're finished registering." She tilted her head toward Díaz.

Rayne took the tablet and filled in her name, email, checked a box for requesting sanctuary, and clicked the submit button. Brief charm magic flashed.

She handed the tablet to Díaz, who had retreated into

watchful silence. His face gave nothing away as he completed the form.

With his abundant magic and indeterminate heritage, he probably excelled at going unnoticed in the mundane human world. Maybe even in the magical world.

She, on the other hand, had to consciously work to keep her eyes from straying to him, or her feet from inching closer, or brushing against him, all aided and abetted by her inner wolf. None of which was even close to professional agent behavior.

She turned to Deputy Hammond, who smelled like a feline shifter. "Any restaurants open yet? We need..." She trailed off when two tall men stepped out of the back hallway. One was a ruggedly handsome, brown-skinned man with strong native cheekbones and jaw. He wore his raven-black hair pulled back and a sheriff's star on his wide, muscular chest.

The other man was the same height and of East Indian descent, and pretty enough to be on magazine covers. He wore tailored, gray slacks and a subtly embellished oxford shirt in flamingo pink. He stepped forward and nodded to both her and Díaz.

"You're late." He nodded respectfully to Díaz. "Impressive work in the auction house takedown."

Rayne sighed. "Brooker, meet Díaz, with the Wizard Imperium. He stopped the hellfrog from eating your strike team. Díaz, meet Florinel Brooker, Investigation Division Chief for the Shifter Tribunal, and my boss. What am I late for? And how did you know I'd be here?"

"Oracle." Brooker made a beckoning gesture that indicated the hallway behind him. "Come with me. I have a project for you. Both of you, if you're interested, Díaz."

Rayne's temper snapped. "Go to hell."

Brooker looked startled. Díaz made a noise that could

have been choked laughter. Hammond busied herself with something behind the desk.

Rayne narrowed her eyes. "I just spent two months in underground hell, got beaten to death, got resurrected, lost my sister, fought off a hellfrog, bounced off a mountain, and haven't eaten in five days." She tilted her head toward Díaz. "Recruit the wizard. He's clever. Recruit the fucking hellfrog, for all I care. They're indestructible. I'm on leave starting now. You'll get my operation report when I get around to it, because you obviously don't need it."

She whirled and strode toward the entrance. She'd seen several restaurants on the carpet ride into town. One was bound to—

"I'll order a pizza," Brooker said loudly.

Rayne thrust her middle finger in the air and kept walking.

"Ma'am," said the other man, his voice low and resonant as thunder. "We haven't been introduced. I'm Sheriff Tanner Stands In River. Call me Tanner. Want me to shoot Flory? Might teach him some manners."

She turned and stopped, amusement bubbling up despite her annoyance. "Nah, he just bleeds and swears."

Díaz's mouth started to curve upward. He turned it into a cough.

Brooker waved impatiently. "Fine. I'll get a luxury suite at the casino and order room service. You can eat while you listen."

She liked and respected her boss, but he was still a work in progress as far as people skills. He'd lived for centuries as his beast, and it showed.

"Food first, and Díaz gets a suite, too. He saved a lot of shifters. And some of those words better be 'well done, Rayne' and 'we'll find your sister,' or I'll shoot you again myself." She put her fists on her hips and glared.

Brooker, seeing all eyes on him, threw up his hands in surrender. "Okay, okay." He slid his phone out of his pocket as he turned to Tanner. "I won't be needing your conference room after all, but you're welcome to come with us."

"Thanks, but I'll pass." Tanner shook his head. "I've got the aftermath of the Fort LeBlanc skirmish to deal with, plus fourteen newly-freed hyenas requesting sanctuary." He snorted. "That's on top of Rorabek throwing orders around like he's the Fairy War Leader of the Western Hemisphere."

"Fort LeBlanc?" asked Díaz.

"Sanctuary town in Canada," replied Tanner. "Vanished in the nineteen-thirties, suddenly reappeared five days ago. Kotoyeesinay honored the original treaty and helped them fight off an attacking army with pillaging on their agenda."

Brooker glanced at Díaz. "An army of wizards." His tone invited a response.

Díaz simply nodded and said nothing.

She didn't blame him for not trusting strangers. Tanner was an enigma. Brooker's personal integrity was rock solid, but she couldn't say the same about some in the Shifter Tribunal, or the organization itself.

She peered down the hall. "Public bathrooms?"

"They're just past my office. I'll show you." Tanner's gesture invited her to follow.

On her way past Brooker, she caught his eye. "If you want Díaz to listen, order some cookies."

10

Arvik's calf ached and his clothes stank, but the world seemed a better place on a stomach full of good food.

He would never have guessed the small mountain town boasted an exclusive casino and hotel. The concierge didn't bat an eye when Brooker ordered dinner and breakfast for a party of six to be sent to the tastefully appointed Grand Teton penthouse suite.

To Arvik's expert senses, the facility glowed with powerful, subtle magic. Which made sense, since it appeared to cater to monied players of any species. That included normal humans who had no idea some of their fellow gamblers were creatures of myth, legend, and nightmare. The casino's magic hid the truth from the wealthy humans, and deterred the non-humans from using their own magic to cheat the humans or the house.

Arvik savored his tender rack of lamb, when he wasn't rebuilding his layered illusion of being a human wizard, or being riveted by Rayne's ever-changing scent. Her natural charisma and unwillingness to take disrespect from anyone

—including him—left him constantly aware of her. Constantly wanting her.

To Brooker's credit, he relaxed and enjoyed his breakfast. His considerable free magic hid whatever animal shared his soul. Undoubtedly why he'd risen so high in the Shifter Tribunal.

Rayne relented her prohibition against talking business once she'd plowed through most of her plate of prime rib and side dishes. She gave Brooker the executive version of what had happened in the underground facility after the strike team left. Interestingly, she didn't mention the auctioneer's tablet she'd found, and didn't correct Brooker's assumption that he was merely a talented human wizard.

Brooker took his empty plate to the tray on the sideboard, then sat back down at the table. "Magister Díaz, I must ask you for a pledge of discretion in what I'm about to disclose."

Arvik straightened his unused silverware with Arturo Díaz-like precision. He considered refusing and walking away, but he was reluctant to leave Rayne, and curiosity won out over his bone-deep weariness. "I so pledge, unless I think it puts the Imperium or anyone I care about in jeopardy."

Brooker frowned, but nodded. "Fair enough. I don't know you, but Rayne trusts you, and I trust her judgment. The Shifter Tribunal has been infiltrated, for lack of a better word, by a faction that believes modern, born shifters are threatened by those that don't fit their criteria." His lips thinned. "After Rayne deliberately got caught, I uncovered strong circumstantial evidence they've been betraying 'impure' shifters to the auction-house hunters to get them out of the gene pool."

Rayne's expression hardened. "Impure, as in changed? Mythics? Latents?"

Brooker's expression turned sour. "Yes, plus those with too much free magic, which I take to mean, more free magic than they have. Even humans with shifter-mate potential."

Arvik raised an eyebrow. "That would explain the high percentage of shifters being offered." He'd wondered about that.

"Let me guess." Rayne's expression hardened. "One of them is Smith, also known as Lingram."

"Yes." Brooker focused on Arvik. "Any idea why he went after you?"

Arvik shrugged. "Opportunity, maybe. I think he was improvising after his original plan failed." He debated mentioning the dart still in his possession, but decided he wanted a sample of its contents first. The magic felt familiar.

Rayne slathered more sour cream on her baked potato. "What about Wong?" She tilted her head toward Arvik. "When she accused him of bespelling me, she complained to Myelle that I'm an 'unregistered' mythic."

Brooker made a disgusted sound. "She doesn't want to kill you, she wants to count you. She leads an international committee that advocates for a formal census and registration of all shifters, especially the rarities. They also want cross-genomic samples."

Rayne rolled her eyes. "Oh, great, let's just give *all* our enemies a map and a checklist." She muttered something about lamebrained politicians. Arvik had to agree.

"Anyway," said Brooker, "We've been monitoring Lingram for close to two years. He's an investment manager for the Tribunal by day, but spends nights on the darker forums under half a dozen aliases, spewing hate and code phrases about disinfectants and cleanups. Surveilling him led us to others of his ilk. He kept a very low profile until recently. When he found out about the planned auction-house raid, he worked all his contacts to get on the team."

Rayne pointed her fork at Brooker. "And you wanted to know why, so you let him."

He nodded. "Myelle's job was to watch him. We should have checked for the weapon." Brooker's mouth twitched a frown. "We still don't know why Lerro attacked him."

"I wonder what set Lingram…" Her words trailed off as she looked at Arvik. "You said the financial records were coming. He tried to shoot you within a minute." She shrugged a shoulder. "Could be coincidence."

Arvik met her gaze. "Or he could be an investor." Both he and Rayne turned to Brooker.

"That's what we planned to ask him, but Lerro got to him first." He blew out a noisy breath. "We don't have time to get a specialist for Lingram, and Lerro is in the wind with the other shifters that escaped."

"Let's cut to the chase." Rayne held up two fingers. "One, the auction house is too dangerous right now. Two, only Díaz knows what I did in the auction house after Myelle left, so maybe I found all the records and haven't turned them in yet. You want to use me as bait to draw out Lingram's pals."

The wine glass in Arvik's hand shattered. He only barely managed to cover his instinctive angry reaction with a look of surprise. "My apologies."

He cleared off a small plate for collecting the larger pieces of broken glass. The cut on his palm stung until he whispered a brief healing spell. It would have healed anyway, but he was supposed to be wizard, not a shifter.

Brooker waved it off, but Arvik didn't miss the speculative look that flashed across his face. Nor did he miss Rayne's tiny hesitation as her fingers deftly pried meat out of the lobster tail and dipped it in butter sauce. He'd better find his lost control quickly, or he'd make a bad mate for her.

That startled him. Since when had he been contemplating a future with her? That was all sorts of impossible.

He shoved the thought aside for later. Right now, he needed his head in the game.

He dampened a paper napkin to pick up the tiny glass shards. "What if I have the records and hold a quick, invitation-only auction for them? You supply the bidder list." Then he could go off the grid and not be distracted by a gorgeous brown-skinned woman and his pushy animals.

Rayne's eyes narrowed, but she said nothing. Smart women were dangerous. And sexy as hell. He wanted to lick the butter off her generous mouth. His animals approved and suggested more things he could lick. This was not helping at all.

Brooker's head tilted. "No offense intended, but what's in it for you or the Wizard Imperium?"

"We still don't know who owns the business. The Imperium can't let them go unpunished, or every corporate cabal will think it's a license to do anything for money, just like the eighties."

He let them think he meant the nineteen eighties, but the worst abuses happened in the eighteen-eighties, when technology and modern magic flourished and lives were cheap. Dark elves who invented hellfrogs and blood-twisted vampires who created zombies had nothing on the obsessive wizard cabals of northern Europe.

He took a deep breath and let it out before his frustration ran away with him. Exhaustion undermined his self-control. "The Imperium can send invitations to their suspects, too. Maybe sweeten the honeypot by saying the records include all bank transactions, to motivate the owners to move their profits before someone comes looking. Big transfers are easier to trace."

Brooker frowned. "Why would they believe you're selling?"

"Wizards are greedy. The assault team thought Ice Age shifters didn't exist until they saw Rayne's dire wolf." He smiled wryly. "They already think I kept her as my prize." *We did*, declared his possessive inner animals with smug satisfaction. He shushed them. "They'd easily believe I've got more to sell."

"We can't stay here." Rayne circled a finger. "The casino is too public, and Kotoyeesinay is a family town. We need a more secure setup location."

Arvik shook his head. "With a satellite uplink, I can be anywhere. Can you lie low for a week?"

Rayne made a dismissive noise. "I'm going with you." She pushed untouched asparagus off her plate onto a side plate, then stood and took it to the trays of food. "You're probably on a mountain-fairy vengeance list."

Brooker's fingers drummed on the table. "She's right. I can supply equipment and transportation, but you need backup. To be brutally frank, we wouldn't trust you on your own. And I'm guessing you wouldn't trust any other agent of ours."

"True." He'd worked alone for centuries because he couldn't trust anyone. Not if he wanted to live.

Rayne knew more about him than anyone and had kept his secrets, which delighted his animals and worried him. He had to consider that mating instincts were warping his judgment. Hers, too, if she felt the mating call. Maybe she was as muddled by all this as he was.

She sat back down with a plate full of fruits and a ramekin of custard. "Where would you go if you *were* selling?"

He started to answer, then closed his mouth. He couldn't believe he was actually considering this. His offer had been meant to keep her safely away, not temptingly close. He'd once secretly dreamed of a life where even monsters had true mates. Over the centuries, he'd put it aside as youthful yearning to avoid his people's lonely fate, but Rayne's effect on him had him questioning the teachings of the tribe leaders. He needed time to think, but as usual, the fates had other plans for him.

He took a deep breath and let it out. "Random locations, random intervals. It's the best way to beat any hired oracles."

Rayne looked to Brooker. "If you're greenlighting this, we need charm-protected tech. I need a nap and Díaz needs a shower and a new wardrobe." She gave him a teasing wink, then turned to her boss with mock ire.

"And for heaven's sake, bring the man some cookies. What kind of luxury hotel doesn't have cookies?"

11

R ayne brushed the snow off the low, flat rock, then slid the heavy backpack off her shoulders and sat. She'd never been to Montana's section of the Rocky Mountains, but they weren't much different from the southern Wyoming mountain she and Díaz had bounced onto four days ago.

He was scouting ahead on four paws, looking for a half-remembered cabin to shelter in for the night, before the coming storm arrived. She usually loved deep wilderness exploration, but she still tired easily, and too many real-world thoughts clamored for her attention.

She worried about how the auction-house cleanup was going, if the shifters who had escaped were safe, including her sister, and whether the honeypot sale of records had attracted the right buyers. The scheduled satellite call to Brooker might be delayed if the storm moved faster than the forecasters thought.

Guilt needled her for not telling her boss about all the files on the auctioneer's tablet. She'd made progress in organizing the jumbled mess of spreadsheets and documents, but she wasn't patient and clever like her sister, so it was slow going.

She'd hoped to get to know Díaz better, but he'd shut her out. Her wolf insisted they were in the mating dance. It felt more like a haphazard tumble down the stairs.

Second-guessing and regrets weren't usually her style, but she wished she'd continued walking out of the sheriff's office. Instead, she'd let her boss talk her into continuing with this phase of the operation. And she'd kept her wolf happy by insisting on staying close to Díaz.

After a too-short nap, she'd met Brooker and Díaz in a hotel conference room to collect gear and a flurry of instructions.

An obliging fairy had opened a portal to an alley in Taipei, and she and Díaz had stepped through, where it was dawn the next day.

They'd found a large hotel lobby and ordered tea while they communed with their respective tech toys. While he set up the auction, she surfed the American media outlets for unusual animal sightings in California. She didn't know if it was good news or bad when she didn't find anything. She spent the rest of the time organizing the messy sales records.

After an hour or so, they wandered out onto the street. With their ballcaps and loose, casual clothes, in addition to the large hiking pack on Díaz's back, they looked enough like jet-lagged American tourists that no one bothered them. His light jacket hid his wide, jeweled wristbands. She bought a new, less glittery tablet cover from a street vendor and ditched Costigan's. He led them to another alley, where he created a narrow portal.

After they stepped through, he looked up and worked a strong spell. From the slightly brighter sky to the west, she guessed they were now in early evening, somewhere in the western hemisphere.

She followed him to wider streets and into a tiny restaurant. It took her a few minutes to realize they were, amazingly, in a small town she knew.

She'd have recognized Cotacachi, Ecuador, sooner if she could have seen the distinctive dormant volcano to the northwest. She'd wondered why Díaz knew it, then wondered if he'd plucked it from her memories, like he'd done before. She'd visited friends the previous year to help build a public veterinary and very private shifter clinic.

No point in asking, because he was back to being Mr. Stoneface McGargoyle. He'd barely said ten words to her, and his selective deafness was better than most felines. She knew how to work with surly, taciturn partners, but she'd expected better from him.

The romantic stories of true mates must have affected her more profoundly than she'd known. Her martial arts training had given her the tools to manage her body's reactions, so it was easier to deal with constantly simmering arousal than her hope.

Instead of looking for a hotel for the night, he led her into a darkened courtyard. After pulling both their parkas out of the backpack and handing hers to her, he opened another portal, this time to a small mountain town, and once again, at twilight. Díaz apparently knew alleys the world over.

They'd walked to a brightly lit convenience store, where she figured out they were in Little Fork, Montana, and listened to the weather report on the loud TV as she shopped.

The clerk came out from behind the counter to watch as she went down the candy and salty snacks aisle.

She put her hands in her pockets and turned to face the pale, weedy man. "Can I help you?"

His chin jutted out as he looked her up and down. "Haven't seen you here before."

She gave him a wide, toothy smile. "Your loss."

He probably would have continued following her around the store, except another customer came in to pay for gas.

Rural towns could be charming, like Kotoyeesinay, but in her experience, they mostly weren't.

Díaz came up behind her, holding a handful of packaged meats and cheeses. "Trouble?"

She turned and shrugged. "Just the usual—shopping while black." Just like visiting some traditional shifter packs, where the crime was breathing while dire wolf.

"Hmm." His face gave nothing away, but his magic flared briefly, like warm fingers caressing her neck. "I think one of the top-ten-best modern advances is electrical power."

A moment later, the clerk cried out in pain. "Son of a bitch! Goddamn thing shocked me."

She smiled. "I love progress."

Outside the store, he opened the map he'd bought and told her to pick a direction. Remembering the oracle problem, she looked away and randomly stabbed a finger at it. Unfortunately, she'd pointed to a rugged mountain top instead of a relaxing hot-spring spa. As soon as they cleared town, he'd handed her the pack and shifted.

That was the last conversation they had for two days, because he spent all but a few moments in wolf form. She followed his path; sometimes, just his scent.

The first night, she'd set up one of the compact tents, ate two packages of ham, and slept as a dire wolf. She was so annoyed with him that she didn't care what he did.

Last night, they'd lucked into a shallow cave to share. He

refused to shift, so she ate the last of the roast beef and cheese, then shifted. He refused to share warmth or even sleep near her. It hurt, but so did a lot of things in life. It was better than being led on with the false hope that he felt anything more than shifter lust.

They'd awakened to a light dusting of snow.

She shifted to human and used her laptop and the satellite uplink to check the weather while she drank a cup of hot tea. An autumn storm was barreling down from the north.

Díaz shifted just long enough to eat a package of tuna and tell her about the high-country cabin that might still be there and the scheduled call with Brooker. Then he'd shifted back to wolf and took off running like his tail was on fire.

She'd decided then and there that out of self-preservation, she had to quit caring what he did or thinking it had anything to do with her. It had been a hard lesson to learn with her father, and it looked like she needed to remember it. It took two willing partners to form a mate bond.

And that didn't even touch on the problem of how such a bond would affect their public and professional lives. Her optimistic inner wolf counseled her to be patient. She smiled sourly. At least they weren't from rival traditional clans, where a cross-species true-mate pairing could break an alliance or start a war. She used to think those were history, until she was sent with a team to Brazil to quell a skirmish that threatened to reveal the existence of shifters. It all started because a jaguar true-mated with a river otter.

Now she sat, sipping from a pouch of water, enjoying the freedom of the high country in the early afternoon light. After weeks of forced inaction in the underground cells, her legs and back felt the strain of nonstop hiking. Thanks to inherent shifter magic, her stamina had improved in the last couple of days, but she needed more healing time to fully recover. She admired full humans who did the same kind of hiking without the benefit of shifter strength or rapid recuperation.

A distant gunshot echoed off the mountain. She'd been listening for hunters ever since she'd noticed that the convenience store sold licenses. Other than hearing the occasional gunshot, they hadn't encountered any close by. She liked guns and approved of hunting to feed a family, but sport and trophy hunting struck her as wanton abuse of the food chain.

Wispy clouds sailed in the dull gray sky over the tops of the scraggly trees. She was out of practice using superior senses and the character of the wind to judge the changing weather.

When she'd been younger, she and her father had been a medal-winning wilderness survival team in the biannual North American shifter games. Then his true mate had died, and in his grief, he'd abandoned both his daughters and thrown himself into long-distance and undercover work for the Shifter Tribunal. Two years ago, he vanished.

A loud canine screech of pain sent ice through her veins. She pulled the backpack onto her shoulders and launched into a fast trot up the divide toward the sound. Her worried inner dire wolf steadied her feet and guided her path.

Another pain-filled whimper made her pick up her pace, leaping over rocks and blazing past the sparse low shrubs.

She rounded the side of a giant, jutting rock and skidded to a halt in a small, flatter clearing.

A natural gray wolf, male from the scent, was caught in a cruel, black iron leg-hold trap. A black chain led from it to a stake that appeared to be drilled into the ground.

She swore in every language she knew and made up new curses to go with them.

The animal saw her and whined in fear as it tried to get away, but the clamp held fast. Blood splattered the snow.

She backed up around the corner of the rock out of his sight. Motherfucking, lazy, greedy, amoral trappers deserved to be caught in their own devices and die painfully of shock or thirst. She'd gleefully help them into the traps.

From the northeast, she felt Díaz's presence coming as fast as a timber wolf could run. He probably thought she'd gotten hurt, the same way she'd worried about him. Her agitated wolf paced inside her mind.

She knew the moment Díaz arrived because the injured gray wolf began growling.

"I'm back here!" No sense assuming he could feel her presence like she could his.

His timber-wolf form rounded the rock and slowed, nose working diligently.

"I'm not hurt. We can talk if you shift."

He looked back toward the clearing, then up to the sky, then at her. The only thing shifting was his fur, ruffled by the wind.

She drilled him with a steely gaze.

"I'm not asking for me. Shift so we can free and heal our little brother. My dire wolf will scare him to death if I go near him."

He sat on his haunches. Several long moments later, the man stood, handsome and infuriating as ever. She couldn't read the flurry of emotions that crossed his face.

"That trap is more dangerous to you than to him." He pointed his thumb back toward the injured gray wolf. "There's a whole string of traps like that between here and the Arctic Circle. They use magic to attract shifters." His expression hardened. "They also count on compassionate shifters to save any natural animal that gets caught, so you get caught yourself."

Rayna swore a vicious oath. "Auction-house wizards?"

He shook his head. "Independent sorcerer-hunters out of Canada. They'll sell to whoever is buying." Distaste crossed his face. "I got a whiff of their magic while we were looking at the weather forecast. I've been tracking it all morning, looking for the trap." He pointed behind him. "Your little brother found it first."

As much as she wanted to have a physical wall-to-wall counseling session with Díaz about his abysmal collaboration and communication skills, the wolf came first.

"How do the traps catch shifters?" She'd rather not discover it the hard way.

"Psychic attractant—makes you see something you can't resist picking up. The trap is actually bespelled Alfar metal. One touch, and you're stuck. Doesn't work on normal humans." He frowned and blew out a noisy breath. "The traps are monitored. They'll know it's been sprung, and they'll know he's an animal, not a shifter."

"Monitored, how? Scrying? Charmed GPS sensor? Spell network?" She frowned. "What's their range?"

"I haven't figured that out yet. I got pulled away from that project last year for the auction-house case."

Her head tilted in thought. "Any spells up your sleeve?"

He shook his head. "My magic is more suited to potential and intent. Portals, electricity, weather, health. I can disable the attractor spell, but it'll take physical shifter strength to open the jaws to free Little Brother."

"I've got a charmed wire saw in my arsenal. Works like a hot knife through butter in human-wrought metals, but it'd take about thirty minutes to cut through Alfar iron."

"Too long. We're already on a countdown." He glanced

to the side. "Here's my plan. You wait here. I'll use my coat to wrap his head so he won't bite. You come hold him while I'll pry open the trap. You run with him back this way, and I'll be right behind you. We'll find a safer place to heal him and send him on his way."

She raised an eyebrow. "Will the sorcerers assume their captured wolf was stolen by a couple of human hunters who just happened to be carrying a pry bar on their wilderness hike?"

"Likely. This is hunting season, and not all hunters approve of traps. The sorcerers won't mess with humans, for fear of the Sorcerers' Guild enforcers."

That comment added a few interesting items to her meager hoard of knowledge about him. "Okay, we'll go with your plan."

She dropped the pack and released the rolled blanket to hand to him. "Use this instead of your coat. Don't get caught by the Alfar metal, because I can't free you. Give me a shout when you're ready for me to hold him. He'll think I want to eat him for breakfast, so work fast."

He started to turn, but she stopped him. "Gloves."

"Right." He pulled them from his pocket as he strode around the rock and out of sight. Confusing, irritating man. At least he was helping the wolf.

She dithered a moment, then slid the backpack on her shoulders. If they had to go a different route, she didn't want to leave it behind.

A long minute later, he called, and she went running.

12

Arvik fought to hold the terrified young wolf still without hurting him. He'd already been bitten twice, hard enough to draw blood.

Rayne dropped to her knees beside him to take the blanket-wrapped head. "Got him."

Arvik angled himself away from the staked chain. "Twist him around."

As soon as she did so, he borrowed the strength of both his beasts to pry open the metal jaws just enough to free the bloody, broken leg. The jaws clanged shut when he let them go.

She pulled back and climbed to her feet, wrestling with the squirming wolf in her arms as she walked quickly away toward the big rock. All shifters were stronger than they looked, but she made it look easy.

Sharp, dark magic flowed from the trap and took the form of an ethereal snake with three heads, each looking a different direction.

Arvik scrambled back and to his feet, throwing a quick

spell to swirl the snow with wind to obscure the spell's vision.

"Run!" He launched himself after her.

He caught up with her in time to catch the pack as it bobbled on her back, threatening to throw her off balance. He steadied it with one hand as they brushed by the rock and ran down the path marked by her footsteps.

Amazingly, even though they were running down a snow-dusted mountainside, healing magic flared from Rayne.

Though it was directed at the injured wolf, she may as well have sent it straight into his pants with sexy intent.

He'd just spent two long days as a timber wolf, trying to gain control over his instinctive attraction to her and the powerful mating drive. Obviously, he'd wasted his time.

Now he was as thick and hard as the upright tree they'd just swerved around. He'd wanted women before, but never like this. He'd better find a way to live with it fast, or he'd be no good to the mission. No good to her.

Meanwhile, she was likely planning his protracted, painful demise for being such an ass.

"Are we far enough?" Her voice stuttered as she ran.

He scanned the terrain and pointed left. "Head for the big burned pine." The ethereal remnants of the lightning strike that caused the damage would interfere with long-range scanning spells.

He bolted forward to scrape the snow off a section of ground below the tree. He cast a visual camouflage spell, in case the spell snakes were still looking for them.

She caught up moments later and set down her whining, blanket-wrapped burden. "I can heal him, but he's so scared, he peed himself. That thing you did with the shifters at the auction house, where you made them listen to you. Can you do that with Little Brother? Tell him we're pack, not killers?"

Arvik ignored the fact that she shouldn't have been able to detect the push from his native gift and considered her question. "Maybe. I'll try." He'd never used it on an animal.

He leaned close to the lump under the blanket that he thought might be the wolf's ear. "You know us." He whispered, compelling the wolf to listen. The usual connection felt different, but there. "We are family. You're safe."

At the suggestion of his darker inner beast, he sang a simple tune he thought he'd long forgotten, of wolf brothers and sisters running free to the sea and back. It calmed both the wolf in front of him and the wolf inside him.

Rayne's healing spell for the injured gray wolf surrounded Arvik like the welcome warm mist from a hot spring. It sparked desire, but also soothed him with comfort and care. Every part of him leaned into that. Maybe that was the trick, accepting the effect of her magic and her warmth instead of fighting it.

He continued singing and loosened the blanket enough to slide a hand up into the fur at the wolf's neck.

Another verse later, and her magic subsided. "That's done it, I think." Her voice sounded low and husky. She rocked back on her heels and stood. "Wait to release him until I'm far enough away." She turned and began hiking up the left slope, adjusting the straps of the backpack on her shoulders.

Arvik used a small wizard spell to clean the urine off the wolf's tail and back legs and the blood off its healed leg. He pulled the blanket away and crab-walked several steps backward, keeping himself low and small.

The gray wolf lay still a moment, then quickly rolled and found his feet. He lifted his newly healed leg then put it down again. Probably natural behavior, rather than marveling at what Rayne had done for him.

The wolf took one tentative step toward him, then another. Arvik pulled off his torn glove, then slowly held out his hand.

The wolf sniffed several times, then bounced back into a crouch, inviting Arvik to play.

It made him smile, but not for long.

"Problem?" called Rayne.

He liked that he could hear her despite the distance and the wind. The charm he'd worn to prevent himself from shifting and breaking his cover while working with the wizards at the auction house had also dulled his superior senses.

He pointed toward the wolf, who danced sideways and yipped. "He thinks I'm his pack. It's a temporary illusion."

"Did you find the cabin?"

"Yes." He stood and pushed his glove into his pocket. "It's two miles northeast. I was coming back to find you when I heard you... Little Brother's cry."

He'd set a wolfish land speed record when he thought Rayne had been caught by the trap that he hadn't warned her about. His list of screwups kept growing.

"Easy-peasy. Lead me to the cabin. If he follows us all the way, despite my dire wolf, shift and go help him find his pack."

"A good plan." He walked up the hill toward her. "Let me carry the pack for a while."

She gave him a bright smile. "Nah, I'm good." Her fingers tightened slightly on the straps.

He started to argue that it was his turn, when it dawned on him that she no longer trusted him with it.

That hurt, but it was his own fault. "I owe you an apology and an explanation."

She shook her head. "No, you don't." She waved to usher him past her. "This isn't your circus. You got suckered by Brooker. His superpower is figuring out how to draw people in. Before you know it, you're sneaking into a war zone for a stolen hard drive, or infiltrating an illegal cage-fight ring, or breaking into a casino vault for incriminating evidence."

He stopped when he got to her and smiled. "Or going undercover in an illegal auction?"

"Oh, no." She rolled her eyes. "That was *my* bright idea. Got my little sister caught, too, and probably scarred Donovan for life." At his questioning look, she added, "Another agent. You knew him as the guard Foster."

Realization hit. He'd noted the same last name in the records without putting two and two together. "Your sister was the other maned wolf, right? Tiny Asian woman?"

"Yep. Different mothers. She's short, kind, and brilliant." Admiration threaded through her words.

The gray wolf had circled warily around them to the right, then bounded up ahead. He paused near the top of the slope and turned to bark at them, as if to complain about their sluggish progress.

Rayne laughed and caught Arvik's eye. "You could shift now, if you wanted. Little Brother would be thrilled. I can follow your scent."

"You can?" Yet another thing that shouldn't have been possible. His shield worked no matter what his form. "I'd rather talk to you."

Of course, maybe she didn't want to talk to him, but by staying wolf, he hadn't given her the chance one way or the other. He vowed to do better.

"Let's talk in the cabin." She pointed up toward the sullen sky. "I like snow and all, but I don't want to be caught out here when the storm hits."

"There it is." He pointed down the slope toward what looked like debris from a minor meltwater flood that got stuck between four boulders.

Rayne's head tilted as a subtle ribbon of magic flowed from her. "Dryad illusion?" She glanced at him. "Your magic, too, and maybe a bit of elven glade. Plus stuff I don't recognize."

"Yes." He murmured the words that unlocked the cascade of concealment spells while admiring her discovery talent.

She smiled. "Bigger than it looks."

He'd discovered a long-abandoned ruin of a hunter's shelter at the turn of the twentieth century and started rebuilding. It was his refuge from the polar fairy and Arctic elf war that threatened to engulf half the magical world. The battleground in Siberia was still recovering.

Her expression turned thoughtful. "You could have ported us straight here."

"No, I couldn't. Anyone who tries to port or teleport to within a few kilometers of this spot gets a random detour to somewhere else. Including me."

Her eyes widened as she smiled. "Impressive. Your design?"

"All except the fairy repellent. I traded for that."

She laughed. "You really don't like fairies, do you?"

"I like them as individuals. I just don't trust them in tribes." He flicked his magic to open the front door. "You're welcome to come in for a tour. The exterior illusion will reset when we go inside."

She glanced at him, then started down the slope. "I'm glad Little Brother remembered his own true pack and took off, or he'd want to live here all winter." She pointed to the covered kennel on the raised porch, sized large enough for a timber wolf.

He laughed. "It and the porch are heated. Want to shift and try it out?"

That made her smile falter. "Maybe later." She climbed the stairs and walked through the doorway.

Another reminder that he'd been making mistake after mistake with her, and he needed to make them right. He tested the quality of the wind with his nose and senses, then followed her in.

She pulled the backpack off and let it drop to her feet as she took in the one big room and loft. "This is fantastic. It's like a rustic version of an ocean world."

Taking pleasure in her delight, he smiled as he shut the door. He took off his coat and hung it on one of the hooks by the door, then sat on the bench to remove his boots, but decided to wait.

She took the backpack to one of the chairs at the café-sized dining table, then pulled off her gloves and stuffed them into the pocket of her dark green parka. "Does the solar panel I saw on the roof provide enough juice to run these, or should I use the battery?" She unzipped the backpack and pulled out their laptops and the uplink.

"We have plenty of power." He crossed beyond her into the L-shaped kitchen and pointed to the four-outlet plate on the outside of the lower cabinet. "Here's a plug."

He flicked magic to unlock all the cabinets, then narrated as he opened several to show her. "Plates and bowls. Dish rack and soap. Dried foods and canned goods. Check expiration dates, though. I haven't been here in five or six years, and stasis spells only go so far."

He opened the valve at the sink, then turned on the faucet. The pipes groaned as the water spurted hesitantly before settling down to a quiet, steady flow. "The tank has a thousand gallons. It's filtered and self-replenishing."

He pointed toward the only interior door, under the ladder that led to the loft. "I'll prime the water in the bathroom. It's a composting toilet and a tiny sink, but the shower is full-sized."

Her fingers traced one of the waves carved into the tabletop. "Did you make all this yourself?"

"Most of it. I've picked up a few trade skills over the years. Improving this place became my hobby." He smiled ruefully. "I'd like to tell you I brought in the big things like the futon and the plate-glass window *before* I anchored the portal block to the deep rock below, but I wasn't that smart."

She moved the electronics to the end of the countertop and plugged them in. "If it's not a touchy subject, how old are you?"

"Five hundred, give or take." He shrugged as if he casually told that secret to anyone who asked. "My people counted seasons."

She nodded. "My father is six hundred fifty something. His people didn't start counting years until the child proved it would thrive, and sometimes, they lost track." She touched the tile mosaic design on the counter. "He'd love this place. He grumbles about the lost art of pretty much everything."

Arvik wanted to ask her why sadness and anger colored her tone, but his instincts said he was on shaky ground with her. She might shut him out entirely if he came across like a spy digging for sensitive information. "He's welcome any time."

Unless her father was a jerk toward his amazingly competent and gorgeous daughter, in which case, her father could go pound sand in Death Valley. Both his animals agreed on that point.

He turned to hide that protective impulse from her. "I'll go turn on the water in the bathroom and start the geothermal heat. We'll have warm water and warm floors in a couple of hours." He circled around the table and headed toward the back.

She opened her laptop and powered it on. "Will your concealment spells let the uplink signal through?" She glanced at the case with the flat, octagonal-shaped crystal. "We could take it outside or put it on the roof."

"Let's test it now. The storm may be trouble. The wind smells heavy with water."

Nodding, she turned back to the laptop.

It only took a couple of minutes to turn on the water for the bathroom and the floor's radiant heat, and pull out soap and towels for general use.

Back out in the main room, he crossed to the entry and grabbed his coat from the hook. His hand was on the door latch before he remembered his vow to be more communicative. "I'm checking things outside."

She waved but didn't look up from her screen.

He rolled his eyes at the unexpected wolfish impulse to present her with a mate gift. He was quite certain she could catch her own mule deer.

13

The custom browser on Rayne's laptop finally finished downloading the animated weather map she'd requested. A warm front collided with the jet stream and formed a dense, white mass coming southeast from the Arctic. If anything, Díaz's instincts about bad weather had been optimistic.

She hoped the call with Brooker resulted in everything they needed so they could finish the project and move on. To what, she wasn't sure.

Her habit of self-reliance usually proved effective, but now, she wished she had more friends, because she needed someone to talk to. The situation with Díaz had her at sixes and sevens with her duty, her common sense, and her inner wolf.

He'd lied to her face and by omission, but all agents lied superbly well, or they didn't live to be fifty, much less five hundred. She was practically a new adult as far as long-lived shifters were concerned, and racked up more new lies with each undercover assignment.

And Brooker had suckered him onto the project. He

wouldn't have done so without knowing more about Díaz than he'd let on, and knowing what buttons to push.

As much as his fantastic scent and his magic tightened her nipples and zinged her core every single time he used it, she wasn't the type to tumble into bed to scratch an itch. Especially not on the job. Absolutely not when it had the potential to change her life forever.

Nothing dissuaded her inner wolf's insistence that the man, timber wolf, and mysterious hidden third animal soul all belonged to her, or dented her wolf's conviction that Díaz and his co-spirits felt equally possessive about her. Dire wolves might mostly live in the moment, but they could be both patient and stubborn when they wanted something. Or someone.

Rayne had heard many tales of mate bonds, but she had to admit she'd never imagined it for herself. Her dire wolf scared most shifters and made some fighting mad. Kind of took the fun and romance out of dating.

A point very much in Díaz's favor was that he found her and her inner dire wolf sexy. She'd scented his arousal and noticed the telltale bulge. And damned right she looked, too, because his firm, muscled body deserved appreciation. In her daydreams, she helped him out of those constricting pants and chest-hugging undershirt, but in real life, she drew the line at seducing a man who'd rather be a wolf.

She missed her sister. Skyla might not know what it was like to be an agent, or have experience with a potential true mate, but she was as smart about people as she was about magic. She'd ask the right questions that would help Rayne figure out what to do.

The cabin's front door opened and Díaz stepped inside. She realized she'd been worried that he wouldn't come back, or that he'd choose to sleep in the heated kennel as a wolf.

She hid her exasperation at her angsty internal drama as she stood and tilted her chin toward the laptop screen. "The uplink works fine for now. You were right. Mother Nature is in a capricious mood. She's probably mad about the whole climate-change thing."

"The cabin's protections should redirect snow drifts, but I brought out the shovels just in case." He'd lost most of the Spanish accent he'd used in the auction house. His natural accent seemed an international hodge-podge that went along with his occasionally poetic phrasing. He pulled off his coat and hung it.

"Sounds good." Watching him made her realize she still wore her own coat. "Are we staying here tonight?"

On his way toward the ladder, he turned. He opened his mouth to speak, then stopped and frowned. "Yes, if the call with Brooker doesn't force a change of plan."

His expression smoothed to neutral and he said no more. Apparently wanting to talk and actually doing it were two different things. Maybe his third animal spirit really was a gargoyle.

"Good to know." She put her cell phone in her pocket, then used the pencil and pad on the kitchen counter to write. "This is my number, but I won't hear it while I'm running. I'm going out while it's still light."

She gave him a sunny smile instead of shifting to her wolf right then and there and biting him. "When I get back, I'll throw something down the hill so you can guide me past the illusion perimeter."

She didn't think he'd leave her out in the cold, but a dire wolf could find a den for the night if she had to.

The backpack mostly had survival food—water, protein, chocolate—and his stuff, so she left it for him and strode to the door. A torn black glove lay on the mat, under his coat.

She scooped it up and tossed it to him. "Good thing you didn't touch the Alfar metal in the trap."

She opened the door and stepped out onto the porch. After a bracing breath of crisp mountain air, she pulled the door shut, then shifted. Giving in to instinct, she shook all over because it felt good, then took off in a fast trot, enjoying everything about being a bad-ass dire wolf.

It had been a snarky way to tell Díaz she'd seen through one of his many misdirections, but he deserved it. Maybe she was lucky he'd been so uncommunicative, so she didn't have to catalog even more lies.

Shaking off the doubts and worries, she gave herself over to her dire wolf to follow her nose to the interesting sounds and smells that caught her fancy. No underground cages, no beat-downs, no disorienting time-zone hopping, no small-town jerks, just the rugged terrain and the whirling wind to rustle through the trees and tickle her fur.

Three hours later, she started down the same slope where Díaz had first shown her the cabin. The setting sun made taller peaks visible even through the storm haze.

Díaz's rocks-and-debris illusion was still damned impressive. Even her discovery magic would have missed it if she hadn't already known it was there.

She shifted to human, keeping the same winter hiking clothes she'd gone out with. She crouched to pick up a small rock and pulled up the hood to keep the steady falling snow from melting down her neck.

When she stood up, the cluttered debris had become a cozy cabin with its back to the mountain. Díaz stepped onto the porch.

Either he'd been watching for her, or his magic defenses alerted him. Her inner wolf insisted he could feel her, the same way she knew where he was. It felt like a natural shifter version of the elven tracker spell her family had used until her father disappeared and she'd broken the connection with her sister.

She let the rock go and started down the slope.

During a pell-mell run through an unexpected U-shaped valley, she'd decided she might not be any better at communication than Díaz. Smiles and teasing banter covered fear, uncertainty, and confusion, none of which agents were supposed to feel, or at least admit to.

Being the best agent she could be had gotten her onto Brooker's team, but more importantly, it had gained her father's approval. That is, once he'd gotten over the shock that she'd applied and accepted the job with the Tribunal without asking for his blessing.

Then he'd vanished, and she'd begun to doubt the integrity of the Shifter Tribunal.

She paused on the porch to brush the snow off herself. Small strips of lights lit the porch and steps, which was plenty for animal eyes to see by.

Díaz followed her in and shut the door. She stifled the impulse to simply turn and wrap herself around him and soak in the feel of his embrace. They owed each other real words first, before they drowned themselves in sensation and need.

The cabin felt noticeably warmer. "The stew smells heavenly." She took off her coat and hung it next to his. "Were you ever a cook?"

His shoulder tension eased. "Occasionally, out of self-preservation. Some people shouldn't be allowed near a cookfire."

She laughed. "Oh, yeah. I knew a woman who could ruin instant ramen."

His sock-covered feet made her realize she was tired of wearing boots, so she sat on the bench to remove them. She lined them up next to his on the mat.

She stood and took a deep breath. "Sorry I was an ass before. I've been in denial about a few things, and you're making me..." She searched for the best way to explain it. "Re-examine my assumptions and priorities."

He blinked, then gave her the first genuine smile she'd seen from him in days. "I had a long apology speech planned, but your version is better."

"Do you want to talk now, or after we eat?" She glanced toward the counter. "Do we still have satellite?"

"Yes to the satellite, and yes to eating first." He waved toward the table, set with plates and glasses. "If we aren't hungry as wolves, we'll be less likely to bite Brooker's head off."

She laughed. "Or each other's."

"That, too."

By tacit agreement they ate quickly and efficiently, without dawdling for conversation. He'd added fresh ingredients and spices to canned stew, and it filled her empty stomach. The yeasty flavor of the fresh rolls made everything taste better.

With thirty minutes to kill while they waited for the appointed time, she helped him clear the table, then visited the bathroom. Her buffalo-plaid flannel shirt, many-pocket vest, and hiking pants were clean enough. She washed her face and ran damp hands over her hair to smooth it back.

After her stint in prison, her hair needed a solid day of pampering. Either the roots needed relaxing, or the relaxed ends trimmed, so she could go natural for a while. Except, thanks to her melting-pot genetic heritage, it tended toward ringlets. She suffered from a near-overwhelming inclination to punch anyone who called her cute.

Díaz was engrossed in his laptop. Rather than stare appreciatively at the muscles of his shoulders and back, visible under his tightly stretched black T-shirt, she took a tour of the cabin's decor. Each artifact contributed to the overall ocean theme, from shaped coral to beautiful, detailed illustrations of colorful fish, to decorated driftwood. The centerpiece was a highly stylized, carved-wood animal in black, red, and white that dominated the back wall. She decided not to tell him it looked like a salmon with legs.

When she passed by the big picture window, she glanced out, then stopped and did a double take.

"Uhm, Díaz? Does your concealment illusion work on natural animals?"

He looked up from his computer. "Arvik."

"What?" She turned to look at him.

"My true name is Arvik Inuktan." He stood, watching her.

She blinked, then smiled. Her inner wolf whined in excitement. True names, true hearts, true mates, as the old saying went.

"It's a pleasure to meet you, Arvik. My true name is Rayne Chekal, but I'm fifty-four, so I'll probably be creating a new public identity one of these days." Maybe he'd tell her later where his name came from. Considering his age and his light brown skin, it was too short and pronounceable to be his original name. "So, your illusion and animals?"

"It should work on anything with eyes and a rudimentary brain. Why?"

She pointed out the window. "Little Brother's back, and he brought all his buddies for a sleepover."

He crossed to stand next to her and look out.

Clearly visible on the dimly lit porch were seven wolf-shaped lumps. Two sat, and five sprawled contentedly on the wood surface, with one half in and half out of the kennel. Snow fell steadily beyond the covered porch.

"That shouldn't…" He shook his head. "I think Lerro must have cast a confluence magic spell on us. Impossible things keep happening."

Like thinking the moon goddess hates you because your true mate is an enemy wizard? Like instinctively trusting him more than people she'd worked with for years? Like suspecting he's a three-souled mythic shifter? That kind of impossible?

"My guess is, your singing magic hasn't worn off." She pointed to Little Brother sitting in the sentinel position near the steps. "The illusion didn't work on him because he ignored his lying eyes and ears and followed his heart. Maybe he influenced the rest of them."

"I don't know what to do." He sounded bewildered and frustrated.

She knew those feelings all too well, especially lately. The impulse to pat his shoulder reassuringly came just ahead of her dire wolf's demand to find Lerro so she could bite him, as a gift to their mate.

She shrugged. "I vote we let them stay until the storm clears. You're the magnet, not your cabin. Once you leave, they'll probably go away, too." She glanced out the window. "If nothing else works, I'll shift, and they'll scatter."

The satellite uplink device sounded a five-note descending chime, followed a few seconds later by a similar sequence that went up, which meant they had a signal again.

Brief magic flared from him, caressing her senses. Her inner wolf sent her a suggestion. *No, I'm not going to nip his ear. He's wearing all those earrings.*

She crossed to the kitchen counter. "It's early, but let's try calling Brooker now, while we still have bandwidth for visuals."

"I agree." He headed toward the room's only upholstered

chair. It was wide enough to hold several substantial pillows and a thick wool throw. Maybe he slept there sometimes, to be near the window. "We can use the blanket for a backdrop."

She turned on her laptop and used her fingerprint to activate the network charm that made the secure connection to the Shifter Tribunal.

He draped the blanket across the backs of the chairs, then sat on the floor. She sat next to him, balancing the laptop on her knees.

She started the software, entered the encryption key, then selected Brooker's icon. The tinny speaker began playing a doorbell every few seconds.

The blanket's tan, white, and azure stripes reminded her of a beach resort in the Indian ocean. "I feel like I'm in a fort with my sister."

His head tilted slightly. "She makes you sad."

She appreciated his diplomacy. "I'm worried about her." She suppressed a sigh, as it was unbecoming of an agent. "I treated her very badly. Even if she's okay when Brooker finds her, she may not want to have anything to do with me."

"My sympathies. It's hard to—"

The laptop bonged with the bright tune that meant Brooker answered their call.

Brooker's nose took up most of the window until he sat back. "You're early." He thumped something out of camera range. The camera jiggled. "I can't see you." He happily embraced technology, but his first instinct was to beat it into submission.

She lifted the piece of tape blocking her camera. "How's that?" She scooted closer to Arvik and angled the laptop so the reference window showed them both in the frame.

Brooker nodded. "Good. Where are you?"

"*Under the sea,*" she sang, a line from the famous musical about mermaids. "How's the auction going?"

Brooker made an equivocal motion with his hand. "Partial success. It's lured in more of the shifter purity crowd. We think they're an investment consortium. Díaz's Imperium contact says they've got some good leads on their end, but none look like owners. Here, I'll show you."

A spreadsheet with names and bids replaced his face.

None of the names meant anything to her, but the bids were higher than she'd imagined.

Arvik shook his head. "I don't recognize the screen names."

The display switched to Brooker's face again. "We're making coordinated arrests tonight during the final countdown. By the way, my office got an untraceable transmission of recent auction-house sales records. You two wouldn't know anything about that, would you?"

"When?" asked Rayne.

"While we were at the hotel. We used some of the files as a 'sample' of the goods." Brooker frowned. "We're keeping the West Coast travel ban in force until we find and help the escaped shifters. If the records are accurate, we've got a lot more missing shifters to track down than we thought."

"And buyers," she said pointedly.

His eyes darkened and became dangerously predatory. "Oh, yes."

And that was why she liked her boss so much.

"Any news about Skyla?" She worked to keep her tone even and professional.

Out of sight of the camera, Arvik's hand brushed her knee. She was comforted by the touch, even if he hadn't meant it that way.

"No, but that's because we've had to back off on the

search. Someone on the same marketplace site we're using posted a bounty for a live dire-wolf shifter."

Arvik stirred beside her. "I believe the Imperium team thought Ice Age shifters were a myth until they saw Rayne shift into her true form." His jaw tightened.

"What happened to your maned-wolf illusion?" asked Brooker.

"Short-circuited by hellfrog blood before I spit it out." She narrowed her eyes to warn him about giving her shit about being more careful. She was as timid as a field mouse compared to some agents she could mention. Like, for instance, the legendary Florinel Brooker.

"Hmph." His mouth twitched. "Anyway, the price is high enough to attract good hunters, so we didn't want to lead them to Skyla with our efforts. Anyway, our oracles are swamped."

"Damn." She blew out a noisy breath. "But thanks."

"In related news, the wizards who attacked Fort LeBlanc all swear their information came from Magister Balton. He swears the orders came from Aldenrud. The involuntarily conscripted shifters we questioned agree."

Arvik nodded. "Aldenrud was embezzling, maybe as his retirement. The earthquake jeopardized his plans. He might have seized on the sanctuary town raid as a distraction to cover his final escape. Your 'board of directors' trick probably scared the life out of him."

"A plausible scenario," said Brooker. "When we find him, we'll ask him how he found out. Fort LeBlanc had only been back two days when he told Balton to pull most of the guards for the raid."

"Hmm." Arvik's expression looked thoughtful. "Aldenrud will be hard to catch. He's a long-range planner. He's flush with cash and has friends everywhere, including fairies with their own pocket demesnes." Arvik's gaze unfocused for a moment. "Maybe check the sales records to see if any repeat customers consistently got bargain deals. The auctioneer would have gone along with it as long as Aldenrud paid her a bonus to make up for her lower commission. She likes thrills and money."

"Good idea." Brooker pulled the pen from behind his ear and looked down a moment. When he looked up, he looked puzzled. "Are you staying with your friends in Ecuador?"

She refused to dignify that with an answer, because he didn't need to know where they were. The question did explain why Arvik had taken them there. She'd bet his burst of magic aimed at the sky was designed to spoof the satellite, and a high-elevation spot might be easier to do it from.

"Never mind. Díaz, do you trust your Imperium contact to help us track down the source of the dire-wolf proffer?"

"I trust my contact, but she's got the same problem you do. Some of her colleagues have hidden agendas. Finding the source might end the immediate problem, but not the long-term threat."

Rayne cleared her throat and glared at the camera. "I hope you're not thinking of sidelining me for my safety. Or because I'm a dire wolf."

Brooker shook his head. "No. You're too valuable." He cocked his head. "But you need to lie low for a few weeks, and nowhere near the West Coast. You're blown as far as the Imperium assault team. I think they used the same marketplace to make sure Díaz sees the offer."

Beside her, Arvik made a disgusted sound. "It's probably a message. They know I have more than one valuable item, and they want a kickback." He frowned. "The New World Imperium is better than it used to be, but they are a fair distance from perfect."

Brooker toyed with the pen in his hand. "No

organization is immune from politics and bad choices." He glanced to his left for a second. "Let's connect again in two days. I'll have the results from the arrests, and the Imperium promises more intel from the Fort LeBlanc investigation."

They arranged the time and details, then ended the call.

She powered off the laptop and the uplink on the kitchen counter while he folded the blanket. She watched him cross to look out the picture window. The man carried himself like a ballet dancer even when he was distracted. No wonder he'd worn heavy boots while in the Díaz persona.

"Snow is still coming down. The pack is still on my porch." He turned to face her. "If you want to leave, we have to do it now, or wait for the storm to pass. Once we get far enough from the cabin, I will port you to wherever you want to go."

Not the talk she'd been expecting. "Do you want me to leave?" It sounded needy, but she needed to know.

"No." He tightened his arms around the blanket. The gem on one of his wristbands flashed with light. "But you may not want to stay."

Smothering her rampant imagination and quelling her agitated wolf, she crossed her arms and leaned her hip on the counter. "Okay, I'll bite. Why not?"

He leaned sideways to put the blanket on the chair. "Because of what I am, and what I'm not. I am a magician, a spy, a loner, a liar, a killer. I am a monster."

He took a deep breath, then let it out in a rush. "What I am *not* is a shifter."

14

Arvik watched Rayne take in his words. His inner beasts stayed stalking still and silent.

She shrugged one shoulder. "You're an agent. Most of that is the price of admission." Her eyes closed for a moment. Then she lifted her chin and caught his gaze. "What kind of monster?" Her fingers splayed briefly. "My inner wolf says you *are* a shifter, albeit one with three souls, which might make you mythical."

His inner beasts urged him to agree.

Unexpectedly, she batted her eyes and coyly proffered the back of her hand. "But I haven't seen everything this wide world has to offer."

It sounded like a quote from a silent-film melodrama. Her simpering smile and high-pitched, breathy tone made him smile in spite of himself.

While she'd been out running, he'd decided to start at the beginning and work his way up to the harder parts. "Do you know anything about the legends of the human First Peoples, or any of the shifter clans up north?"

"Sorry, no. Classrooms made me bitey. You're lucky I

know they don't call themselves Eskimos."

His noisy beasts pushed him to blurt everything out at once, to kiss her, to whisk her away to the beach and show her. He compromised by inviting her to sit with him at the table.

"In our legends, the shamans of two starving shifter clans in the Arctic used powerful, dark arts to become one people. They became more than shifters with the strengths of man and beasts, with extra free magic. They conquered all other tribes, human and shifter, in the north. They called themselves the Ulu, the sharp knives, but came to be known as the Ahklut, after the male who named himself chief of all the Ulu bands."

"When was this?"

"Depends on who you ask. My grandparents said twenty thousand years ago. Others put us as far older, but that might be more fable than fact."

"We shifters love legends, don't we? My favorite philosophy professor said it's because we know less about our origins than any of the other magical species." She smiled ruefully. "Sorry. So, the Ahklut clan was the terror of the north."

"Yes, for centuries. When Ahklut himself died, successors took up the spear. By the time I was born in the early 1500s, as Europeans count it, the Ahklut were in decline, down to maybe a few thousand on three hidden islands. Children were rare, and healthy children rarer still. A famine drove food animals southward. The shifter and human tribes followed, but the Ahklut could not. According to our teaching tales, one of the costs of our merge was a fatal intolerance to warmth."

Her finger traced the wing of the thunderbird figure he'd carved on the table. "Does your magic protect you?"

"Yes." The lie rolled off his tongue before he caught it.

"Not anymore." He forced himself back on track. "We had no other skills beyond ravaging and pillaging. Everyone went on raids. Male, female, old, young. Only the injured or females nursing younglings stayed home. Our native gift, the charisma magic that made Little Brother our best buddy, compelled shifters and humans alike to listen. Our nature is trouble, and fear is our weapon. We took what we wanted, when we wanted, because we could. Our magic was undetectable, unstoppable."

A corner of her mouth twitched. "Except by polar fairies, perhaps?"

He snorted. "True enough, but neither they nor their age-old enemies, the Arctic elves, cared what we did as long as we left their glades and demesnes alone and didn't reveal their existence to humans. The northern forest giants ignored us, and we ignored them. Thunderbirds killed us on sight. That's what happened to my parents. But there weren't enough of them to chase us all over the Arctic."

"So, what changed?"

"Politics. I grew into a tall and fierce fighter. I had more free magic than most, though I didn't know how to use it. The clan's most powerful and ambitious shaman sought to use me as his instrument to control the chief and thereby, the clan. But I had already been shaped by my grandparents as a weapon in their secret crusade for peace."

Her eyes widened. "Wow." She smiled. "Do you have any popcorn? This is getting good."

Amusement bubbled up out of him. "No." He hadn't realized how much he'd missed having someone to laugh with until he'd met Rayne. "A serious oversight on my part."

"I'll start a shopping list." She grinned. "Go on."

"My grandparents raised me after my parents died on a raid. They were part of an underground pacifist faction that was gaining popularity as the old raiding ways failed. They taught me compassion and helped me figure out how to use my magic to defend and heal. By the time Nu'untivut, the shaman, realized I would never be his weapon, I was too visible and well-liked to kill me outright. I'd become the face of the radical notion that the pitiless, rapacious Ahklut could embrace the way of the original three-spirited Ulu, who could trade instead of take, cooperate instead of command."

She rested her chin on the heel of her hand. "Ahead of your time?"

He nodded. "Fear of change, too. I was young and idealistic, despite the countless raids I'd been on and the people I'd hurt. It took five unexpected deaths of my friends and allies for me to realize it wasn't just bad luck." He pushed aside the old memories of blood on the ice. "Then Nu'untivut murdered the old chief and assumed clan leadership, as no previous shaman had done. He demanded loyalty from all, but took counsel from none. Only I was left to oppose him. With few friends left, I couldn't protect my family. I killed his strongest, most vicious fighter in a public fight, then fled south forever."

"That had to be hard. I was never in a pack, but I can't imagine what it would be like to leave everyone I ever cared about behind. Even if I was forced out."

Her other hand had drifted closer to his on the table as she spoke. He wanted the connection and comfort of her touch, but he forced himself to ignore it. He still had so much to tell her.

"It was hard, but the alternative was worse. I was lucky. Magic got me out of trouble and kept me cool." He showed her one of his wristbands. "I saw my first desert and my first jungle. I learned to hide my nature from shifters and magic users, the ancient races, and even mirror mages and oracles. I studied more magic when and where I could, and learned more mundane medicine when it advanced beyond wishful thinking and blood-letting. Spying came naturally. I'd already learned fitting-in as a survival skill. I love learning secrets. I still believe in doing what's right. I've tried to atone for what the clan did. What I did." He shook his head. "Sometimes, I make a mistake and take a job with the wrong people. That's how I ended up on a team of greedy wizards who think I'm like them."

"You are an excellent spy. But they're morons." She waved her hand dismissively. "So what happened to your people? I think I'd have heard about a clan attacking shifter communities."

"I don't know. I've spent the last four centuries avoiding the northern latitudes and pretending I knew nothing of the Ahklut. In the mid-1800s, I heard rumors that part of the clan split and settled in Siberia." He made a face. "Until now, I've never wanted to go back. If my grandparents are still alive, Nu'untivut or his successor would kill them to hurt me."

She raised an eyebrow. "Until now?"

"You said it better than I did, earlier. I've been re-examining some fundamental assumptions about myself, because the last few days have proved them wrong. *You* proved them wrong." He laced his fingers together to keep himself from reaching for her hand.

She said nothing, but her warm expression invited him to continue. Honesty was a novel experience.

"Ulu lore says our native gift of charisma magic is supposed to be undetectable, but you felt it, back in the auction house. I think Lerro did, too. It's not supposed to work on animals, so I never tried until you asked. Now I have a wolf pack on my porch."

She quirked a teasing smile. "They scented your stew."

"Sure, once they slid right by the cabin's magical

defenses." Which he'd forgotten to set, because he'd only cared that she came back from her hike.

Her head tilted toward the door. "Should we check for more visitors?"

"No, it's my fault. Detection spells only work if you activate them. The spells registered the wolves as invited guests. We have no others, invited or otherwise."

"It's hard to balance security by obscurity and deterrence sometimes." She pushed back her chair and stood. "Water?"

"Please." He watched in case she needed a reminder, but she went straight to the correct cabinet. "When I went south, I used magic to keep cool for the first few decades after I left, but I eventually found I didn't need it. Either I acclimated through magic, or heat intolerance is another tale of dubious origin."

She filled the mugs with cool water and brought them to the table. "What else?"

He picked up his mug as she sat. "In my clinic, I was able to direct your own free magic to heal you. Ulu magic is supposed to be incompatible with real shifter magic, like oil and water."

"I'm glad you busted that myth, then." She shook her head and thinned her lips. "Donovan—the guard Foster—had to help 'kill' me and convince the others I was dead. I had a mission to complete, and it was the only way Skyla would leave without me. My discovery sense told me heavy things were coming down at the auction house, and I didn't want her to be a casualty." She sighed. "I should have found a better way."

"Sometimes, there are only different ways, not better." He circled the rim of the water glass with his finger. "You shouldn't have been able to tell that I was anything but an arrogant wizard, or at most, a simple timber wolf. My shields have fooled nosy magic users and ultra-suspicious shifters for centuries, or I'd have been dead a hundred times over."

"Simple wolf, eh?" She chucked. "Like I'm a shy maned-wolf." Her smile faded. "So why do you want to go back to your people now? Assuming they're still around."

"Answers. Unfinished business. Family." He blew out a loud breath. "I've been hiding alone in the shadows for five hundred years. I think I might like the sunlight."

His courage faltered. Giving up any more secrets meant he'd have no shield, no net, and a charred bridge behind him. He took a slow sip from his mug.

Her shoulders hunched slightly. "I have a theory that might answer some of your questions, but you might not..." She trailed off. "It will change things." Her finger pointed back and forth between them.

He hadn't heard vulnerability in her tone before. Admittedly, he'd only known her for ten days, and she'd been unconscious for four of them, but it caught his attention. "I'm willing to risk it if you are."

Her gaze caught his and held it. "I could be immune to your magic because both my wolf and shifter magic say you're my true mate, and that I am yours."

A flash flood of wonder threatened to sweep him away. Both his animals surged forward at once. He clenched his jaw tight against their desire to take control of his words.

She sat up in her chair, her face neutral, but her posture stiff. "My apologies. I won't mention it again."

He shook his head, sorry that he'd hurt her, frustrated with himself. "Our origin tales all say that in becoming the Ulu, we lost the blessing of the true-mate bond. For five hundred years, I believed it. Then I met you."

Her expression didn't change.

He took a deep breath and let it out slowly. "My animals

insist you are our mate, even though it's supposed to be impossible. I feel your presence, even when you're kilometers away. Your touch sets me on fire, and your magic makes me want to find out if you taste as different as your scent each time I kiss you. I want to blast anyone who looks at you with greed or disrespect." He stood up and paced a small circle behind his chair. "I spent two days as a wolf, trying to get control of myself. It didn't work. You probably wanted to push me off the first steep mountain we came to."

A corner of her mouth twitched. "Maybe the second mountain."

"I'm sorry I was a jerk. I didn't talk because I didn't know what to tell you." He shook his head. "That's a lie. I was afraid to tell you."

"Me, too. I feel everything a shifter mate is supposed to feel. The primal need to join with you, mentally and physically. Even your breathing is sexy. Your magic makes me want to lick you everywhere, and your scent..." She inhaled and splayed her fingers like an explosion. "Wow."

She stood to face him, then slid her hands into the pockets of her vest. "But bodies want what they want without worrying about the consequences. Dire wolves live for the now. Golden strands of shifter-mate magic are potential, not destiny." Her gaze dropped, then met his again. "I planned to kill you because you were a wizard who sold shifters like cattle. Then I thought I'd have to kill you because you were a *shifter* who sold other shifters. Not a golden start to a successful relationship." She shook her head. "But you freed me and all of us instead of saving yourself. You stopped a *hellfrog*. You offered to hold the fake auction because you wanted to protect me. You helped me save Little Brother." Her lips curved upward. "You zapped the convenience-store clerk."

"Any time." He was mesmerized by her mouth and frozen by the fear that if he moved, hope would vanish.

She tilted her head. "I'm still not getting the monster part."

"My third spirit is not found in nature." He pointed his chin toward the large and bold Northwest Coast aboriginal art piece on the back wall of the cabin. "That comes closest."

She turned to study it. Suddenly, she saw it for what it was. "You're an orca? A killer whale?"

"Maybe we were once. We've got the coloring and the shape, but we're bigger. We have limbs and claws where fins should be. We use them to climb out of the water and shift to wolf or human."

She grinned. "I'd love to see you." Her hands fluttered. "If you're willing."

"Yes." His new policy for honesty made him continue. "I want to hunt with you, swim with you, spend a week in bed with you. Make you laugh. Find out if you like sashimi. Learn how you do that thing with your wardrobe. Help you find your sister." He locked his knees against the desire to take the few steps that would put them in touching distance. "But not until I track down my people and find out the truth. You and I both need to know if I can form the bond that real shifters do."

After several long moments, she nodded once. "I hear you. My wolf is already shredding me for just thinking of letting you go without us to protect you." She rocked back and forth on her heels. "But neither of us is in the right line of work for a normal courtship, and we both have unfinished business." She snorted. "Every mating dance is unique, but I wouldn't know normal if it wore a nametag."

He hissed dismissively. "Normal is for statisticians. This is just us." He took a deep breath and let it out fast. "I have to tell you, not touching you is killing me."

"We could try another hug." She opened her arms in invitation and gave him a smartass smile. "Maybe this time, we won't land on a tree outside of Kotoyeesinay."

Within a heartbeat, he wrapped her in an embrace. He expected the hot, tingling desire—his constant companion for the last week—but the comfort that washed through him took him by surprise. Had he been in that much pain? His inner beasts settled and leaned into the feeling of her face resting on his chest. The feeling of home.

He dropped his head to draw in a full breath of her scent. This time, it was lemon, dust, and wet feathers, with an undercurrent of pure feminine arousal. He took another shuddering breath.

"See? You're sexy just breathing." Her arms tightened around him. "I've never wanted anyone like I do you. If we kiss, I'll never want to stop."

Even nuzzling her hair was sensuous torture. "Sorry, no brains for words. All my blood is going here." He ground his hips into hers, letting her feel his hard arousal.

She groaned and met his thrust with her own. "I'm aching for you." Her embrace loosened and she looked up. "But we're playing with an open campfire in a drought-stricken forest."

He reluctantly released her and took a tiny step back. "Yes." He took another deep breath, forcing himself to think. He couldn't remember why they couldn't just give in to the pleasure.

Unexpectedly, his usually distant and taciturn orca came to his rescue. *Because we must give her everything so she can heal us.*

Everything meant the true-mate bond. His journey to the past. He took another small step back. "What's your unfinished business?"

She dropped her hands from his hips, but caught one of

his hands with hers. "The sales records."

Right. Her mission. The auctioneer's tablet that he knew she still had because he'd seen her with it in Taipei. "How did you get a copy to Brooker?"

She smiled. "I shifted in the restroom so I could retrieve the tablet. I asked the Kotoyeesinay sheriff to copy the hard drive and told him to send it anonymously to the investigation division." Her eyes drifted a little as she frowned. "You might want to stay well shielded around him."

"Why?" He had to admit the big man had made him wary, not his usual reaction to a pleasant stranger.

"He's another Ice Age shifter. A teratorn. What Native Americans called a thunderbird."

His eyes widened. "They're still around? I heard they got wiped out by colonization."

"Yeah, which gives me hope that your people might still be around, too." She turned and gently tugged on his hand. "Let's check the weather and the kids."

He followed her to the large window. The snow had mostly stopped, but the wolf pack was still there, sprawled like lazy hounds. The young male with the distinctive blaze on his tail, the one Rayne had named Little Brother, lay recumbent near the kennel. He looked up at them through the window, then put his head back on his paws and closed his eyes.

"Do you like children?" she asked.

"Yes." He had to remind himself the honesty policy was still in force. "But I've never lived with them, never hoped to have my own. Ulu can't…" He trailed off. "I was about to say, 'breed with outsiders,' but that might be yet another myth." How was it he'd always been so keen to learn hidden truths about everything and everyone but himself?

"Since I'm guessing that you've had plenty of sex with

fertile females more than a few times in four hundred years of nomading around the globe, it might be true."

He didn't know how he felt about children, if he was honest with himself. "Does it bother you?"

She smirked. "What, that if we win the true-mate lottery, we might not have pups, or that you had lots of sex with lots of other people?" Her fingertips stroked the stubble of his beard. "I'm not the jealous type. If I was, I chose the wrong career." She gave him a soft smile. "I hope you have had some loving relationships, because five hundred years is a long time to be lonely. And as to kids, I love other people's children because I can give them back. Let's see how we feel about it in, say, another fifty years." Her fingers moved to the corner of his mouth. "Meanwhile, I think I'd like to take a chance and see if I can kiss you just once."

He tilted his head toward hers, then hesitated. "What if we can't stop?"

"Oxygen. We have to come up for air." Her lips met his.

He settled her into his embrace and teased her with his tongue. She sent her tongue out to play, then opened and invited him in.

An involuntary moan came from him as her taste, primordial and sweet, sent lightning through his blood. She circled her hips across his rock-hard erection, nibbling gently on his bottom lip. He clutched her fantastic, muscled ass and pulled her tight against him.

Minutes or hours went by before she broke off the kiss with a deep gasp, her chest heaving. "How soon can we leave?"

He caught his own breath. "Thirty minutes, if we don't let sleeping wolves lie"—he tilted his head toward the porch —"and we're willing to hike through the snow in half moonlight. Why?"

"I'm about two seconds from jumping your bones." Her

palm flattened on his chest. "The sooner you find your answers, the sooner we can choreograph our own courtship, whether or not it involves a mate bond."

Covering her hand with his own, he touched his forehead to hers. "You are a remarkable woman."

"I'm not, but don't tell my boss. He thinks I walk on water." She looked up at him with a twinkle in her eye. "Can your proto-orca do that?"

He laughed. "Proto-orca? No, I'm too heavy."

She cupped his face in her hands. "We don't say 'heavy' these days. We say 'curvy.'"

He frowned in mock outrage. "Orcas are not curvy."

"Whatever you say." She spun away. "Come on, hottest not-shifter-man on the planet. I'll pack the gear we came with. You close down your cabin."

As he put away dishes, sealed cabinets with stasis spells, filled water pouches, and shut off the heat and water, his inner animals voiced their extreme displeasure at letting her out of their sight, especially without mating her first. But like she'd said, animals only dealt in present tense. It was up to him to plan for the long game.

Twenty minutes later, he stood in the middle of the cabin and reset the last of the spells that would keep the cabin hidden and safe. His winter clothes felt too warm, but he'd be grateful for them outside. According to the satellite weather map, the autumn storm had veered east, but left howling winds in its wake.

Rayne zipped her boots and stood. She'd changed into a white hooded coat and light grey snow pants from her seemingly endless wardrobe. And arsenal. She now carried a shotgun in a holster slung across her back. Anyone who noticed them would likely take them for night hunters. It was the little details that counted.

He pulled on the gloves he'd mended with a little magic.

"When we get beyond the distortion boundary, where do you want me to port you to?"

She stomped each of her feet, as if seating them in her boots. "What's the cost to you? You're phenomenally gifted, and you would totally get a kick out of my prodigy sister, but all magic is finite."

He clamped his mouth shut before the usual evasions rolled off his tongue. She wasn't the enemy, trying to probe his weak spots. "Distance is the key. I can do six or eight local ports in a day, within twenty kilometers or so. The three global ports I did after Kotoyeesinay were my limit. Left me with a scorching headache for hours, even after I shifted."

She shrugged one shoulder. "May as well visit the mothership." The corner of her mouth twitched teasingly. "Know any good alleys Chicago?"

He smiled, amused that she'd noticed his pattern. "One or two."

"Any idea how long your search will take?" She held up her hand and rolled her eyes. "Sorry. Forget I asked. It takes what it takes. But don't go Stoneface McGargoyle on me again, or I'll find Lerro and use his oracle visions and confluence magic to hunt you down."

Strong, confident women had always been his treasure. "I may be old and slow on the uptake, but I can learn new tricks." They'd agreed to start with a message drop service located in Kotoyeesinay, then skip randomly to others. "You stay in touch, too."

"Deal." She strode up and gave him a searing kiss, as if memorizing him. "You're not old and slow." She patted his chest. "You're experienced and deliberate."

He bared his teeth in a mock snarl and allowed his wolf to shine through his eyes.

She laughed, licked his nose, and twirled away.

15

Rayne carefully placed one paw forward, then another, testing each spot for sticks or leaves that would crunch under her weight. She might look like a prize borzoi, but the illusion didn't compensate for the extra heft of the real dire wolf underneath.

She silently cursed the clear late-November night and the full moon. She'd be too noticeable crossing the manicured front lawn, so she was forced to creep through the shrubbery between the main house behind her and her target, the cabana. It had been styled to look like a miniature Athenian acropolis standing in front of a heated three-level pool. Fortunately, the icy breeze deterred late-night swimmers.

She was back on the job as a covert agent, working with a partner for this particular mission. They had already completed the objective of drilling a security hole through the party host's computer network. The Shifter Tribunal cyber specialists were probably already exploiting it to track down the locations of captive shifters. The mansion owner, a witch, had acted as a buyer's agent. His fondness for conspicuous excess, debauched parties, and pricey eternal-youth spells made him a worthy target. Cracking his records would help the Tribunal track more lost shifters.

The diamond-studded collar around her neck beeped. *"The chef noticed my precious baby isn't in the mudroom anymore. I told her I let you out to do your business and you went after a rabbit. You've got maybe five minutes until they get someone to help me look."*

Rayne softly yipped twice to let Myelle know she got the message.

No more time for subtlety. She bolted out of the bushes like she was flushing the rabbit and sped up the steps, past the cabana's pillars, onto the porch.

She slowed and followed the recent scent trails that led to the set of sliding glass doors. Magic didn't come as easily in her dire-wolf form, especially when she was wearing an extra illusion, but her sensitive nose told her plenty.

She touched a paw to the glass. Fairy magic, coming from inside. Her dark-adapted eyes detected multiple doorways.

Instinct said to move. She jumped off the porch into the bushes and ran toward the house as if she'd seen a ghost. Just as she rounded the corner, the back door opened. A stunning brown-skinned woman wearing a feather boa and a dress of connected doilies stepped out in stacked stiletto heels, followed by a large gray-suited white man brandishing a flashlight.

"Thank you for helping me." Myelle simpered better than a Civil War southern belle, and she didn't even need the accent. "She's usually a very good girl, but when she's in heat..."

The man looked annoyed as he swept the small patio and walkway with the flashlight's beam.

Myelle shivered and crossed her arms, plumping up her cleavage. "Anastasia! Come to Mama, baby!"

Rayne barked excitedly and made a mad dash straight for Myelle. At the last second, she dodged aside, then crouched, inviting Myelle to play.

Myelle patted her thigh. "Come here, you naughty girl."

Rayne obligingly stuck her cold nose on Myelle's exposed skin, then snuffled wetly. It was fitting revenge for the "in heat" comment.

Myelle snapped a glittery leash on Rayne's collar. "I think it's time for you to go home, young lady. You're obviously not on your best behavior tonight."

Rayne whined and dropped her head in canine remorse.

Myelle led the way into the warm house and beamed cheerfully at the few people who were still on their feet. "We found her."

"Tha's good," mumbled a human woman in red, weaving as if she stood on a rocking boat.

The vampire next to her put his arm around her waist. He didn't look happy.

Myelle turned to the hulking man. "Can you have my car brought around?" With a gesture that bordered on theatrical, she flared magic, and her feather boa morphed into a floor-length painted velvet opera cloak. "It's the blue SUV with big kennel in the back."

"Yes, madam." He sent a text message on his phone. His long-suffering expression morphed into relief. He'd likely assumed his security gig would entail battles, not bellhop duty. "The valet will deliver it to the front door in a few minutes."

Myelle slowly worked her way through the room, chattering happily with whoever was unimpaired enough to carry on a conversation. Rayne sorted through the scents and wolfed down half the contents of an unattended tray of brie-and-salmon appetizers before Myelle caught her.

Under the porte cochere at the front of the big house, Myelle tipped and hugged the valet when he handed over the key. She opened the SUV's back gate and the kennel so Rayne could jump in and lie down like a good dog.

Once on the road and well away from the estate's entrance, Myelle pulled into a darkened driveway long enough to swap her outfit for comfortable exercise clothes. Rayne shifted and put on similar gear and climbed into the passenger side.

Myelle's gold-tipped fingernails tapped on the steering wheel in time to the energetic swing-band classic coming from the speakers. "Why the cabana?"

"I heard someone say it's a front for a fairy demesne." Rayne unhooked the charmed diamond choker that shifted with her.

"And?"

"Not enough time to confirm." Rayne disliked shading the truth with Myelle, but the existence of the demesne was the first bright spot in a month of frustrating disappointments. She wasn't sharing the lead with the Tribunal until she got to use the information first.

The first two weeks after leaving the Montana mountains had gone well. She'd rented a private townhouse in Chicago, napped often, used the Tribunal's amazing gym to work out her frustrations, and eaten everything in sight. Arvik looked equally rested on video when he called Brooker and her two days later. The shifter-purity conspirators were awaiting judgment, and the request for a live dire wolf had been withdrawn. After that, she and Arvik had exchanged short messages every other day. His appearance in her dreams helped soothe her alternately irritable and mournful dire wolf. The Tribunal had rescued nearly three hundred shifters from the two escapes and from recent buyers.

But from then on, nothing seemed to go right.

No more hot dreams of sexy Arvik. She couldn't even feel the tiny connection thread anymore. Maybe she'd been fooling herself about that all along.

No news on her sister, except a Tribunal oracle's vague prediction to look to the North Star. Lerro was nowhere to be found, but the shifters he'd led to freedom were all safe.

Families and clans had been ripped apart, and some would never recover. Four years of auction-house sales meant an appallingly high number of shifters were still missing.

The sales records from the auctioneer's tablet had only covered the previous eight months. Rayne's secret project had hit a dead end. Her discovery sense said she was missing something in the files on the tablet, but she'd practically memorized them and still couldn't find it.

The stupidest, slightest things reminded her of her time with Arvik. A sad news story about an orca mother that wouldn't leave her dead calf. A radio ad for a performance by Pacific Northwest aboriginal musicians. The salmon appetizers at the party tonight.

Ordering herself to quit brooding like a soap-opera diva, she turned to Myelle. "Anything interesting happen while I was upstairs or outside?"

"Define interesting." She snorted. "The host's 'best-sex-ever' talismans, which he's selling for a thousand a piece, are glamoured tourist charms from Morocco. The chef is quitting tomorrow because she hasn't been paid in a month. I had more hands-on propositions tonight than I had in six months as a stripper."

"At least we got tips as strippers." They'd met on that case six years before, taking down a syndicate that used the club as a front for smuggling immigrants. Some coyotes would do anything for money.

"And we had bouncers to eject the riff-raff." She wiggled her shoulders, as if shaking something off. "I'll have to take an extra-long shower tonight, or my two mates will be all territorial because I smell like other people."

Rayne looked at her in astonishment. "You're mated?"

Myelle laughed. "You didn't know? You're usually the first to know everything." She lifted fingers from the wheel. "But I'll cut you some slack, since we haven't worked together in three years, and you're allergic to being indoors."

Rayne shook her head. "How do you handle being away from them for months at a time? And how do they handle you being in danger?"

"Roshan is a mythic shifter and firefighter, and Lee is a bird shifter and a test pilot, so they have no room to complain about danger. There's no doubt we're mates, but it took us some getting used to, being part of a triad. Lee is nearly six hundred, and Rosh and I came from very conservative clans—you know, 'one mate, one bond.' My mother still pretends I was switched at birth. And yeah, I miss them like I miss air, sometimes."

"How do you hide the mate bonds?" Every shifter could sense mate bonds, the way humans could smell popcorn. Most of the ancient races could see them if they wanted to.

"The same way you hide your scent and your bad-ass dire wolf. Magic and misdirection." She sighed and glanced at Rayne. "The same way I've been hiding my pregnancy."

Rayne's eyes widened. "You are? That's wonderful!" Shifter births were uncommon and cherished events. She frowned. "And you're still going on undercover assignments?"

Myelle growled. "Pregnant is not disabled." It sounded

like an oft-repeated phrase. She sighed. "But this is my last field trip for a couple of years, because, Goddess help me, I'm carrying twins. I already have a desk job. I'm out with you because I like you and because trafficking in shifters pisses me the fuck off."

"I like working with you, too." Rayne looked out the window as they passed the wide pillars and wrought-iron gate that marked an estate entrance. "Could I talk to you about what mating is like sometime?"

Myelle smiled. "Ooh, Little Wolf, do tell! You got a prospect?"

"Maybe." *Absolutely*, groused her inner wolf. "It's... fraught."

"Fraught?" Myelle laughed. "All matings are–"

An attention-getting series of tones burst from both their Tribunal-issued communication devices.

"This is an emergency recall. Report at once to a code blue twelve portal. Repeat. This is an emergency recall..."

"Check that," Myelle ordered.

"On it." Rayne was already sliding her phone out of her pocket and thumbing it on.

Myelle touched a control in the steering wheel. "Bastet, stop music. Display live navigation."

Rayne entered the encryption code on her phone and aimed the camera at her face for the authentication. After a long wait, the logo appeared, faded, and was replaced by words on the screen. "Recall confirmed."

"Goddamn it." Myelle pointed toward the map now displayed on the console. "Why do stupid witches have to live in the middle of Bumfuck, Nowhere?"

Rayne chuckled. "I don't think the Hamptons qualifies as Bumfuck."

"Bastet, plot fastest route to the Long Island Airport. Deploy radar scrambler." The Tribunal's network of emergency portals included most modern airports. "Ninety miles from civilization is Bumfuck, as far as I'm concerned."

"Depends on whether or not you consider New York City civilized." Rayne tapped menus on her phone. "Here's the full recall notice." She scrolled down. "Shit."

"What?"

Rayne met her colleague's brief glance. "It's war."

Rayne leaned against the side wall of the standing-room-only auditorium. The tiny pocket demesne that contained the auditorium deep in the Shifter Tribunal building had three thousand seats. She'd never seen or smelled so many shifters in one room, not even when she'd been in the auction house.

And not just shifters. Magical humans, elves, fairies, vampires, wraiths, djinn, and representatives of a dozen other ancient species shared the space. Spellcast images allowed even more to be present in spirit.

Triffum, the Shifter Tribunal's new interim president, stood on the dais, eyes cast down at the podium. The bear shifter was older than the hills but still vigorous, and had been drafted specifically because he had no ambition to run anything. The previous president had turned out to be an investor in the buyers' consortium organized by the shifter-purity cabal. No one had seen her since the day before the timed arrests, and her house had burned to the ground that night.

Precisely on the hour, Triffum looked out at the audience. "Thank you for coming." Built-in magic carried his voice throughout the room. "This is the most serious threat to shifters and the secret of our existence—and that of all magical peoples—that we have faced since the polar fairy-Arctic elf war in 1908."

As Triffum spoke, Rayne heard the quiet murmur from translation spells for non-English speakers.

The four giant multimedia monitors above the dais displayed an image of a map of northern Canada marked with a pulsing spot near a river.

"Most of you have heard that nine weeks ago, the long-missing sanctuary town of Fort LeBlanc reappeared. Four nights later, a company of wizards took an invasion force in a bid to take the town." A series of still photographs and short video segments accompanied his words. "They were defeated by the newly awakened town elders and returning citizens, including the crow shifters who took these photos. Because of a long-standing treaty, they were aided by volunteers from the sanctuary town of Kotoyeesinay, Wyoming."

Rayne hadn't expected to see anyone she knew in the images, but she recognized one. She pushed herself off the wall and stood up straight. In the candid photo, a smiling polar fairy wearing battle armor was talking to a serious-faced, tall, well-muscled human who looked like a mountain man. He'd shaved his beard and trimmed his wild hair, but she recognized his build and his eyes. The auction house had called him "Brick," because they'd believed the Siberian tiger's human half was brain-damaged. His real name was Nic, and he'd been smart enough to fool the guards for weeks. More important, he'd last been seen escaping the flooded facility with her sister, Skyla.

The big displays blanked.

Rayne made herself relax and lean against the wall again. One way or another, she would be in the group that went to Fort LeBlanc.

"... reporting another threat to the town. Ordinarily, we would not insert ourselves, but in this case, we must."

For the first time in his measured speech, anger colored Triffum's tone. "Taken as a whole, the predictions point to a deadly enemy that our elders remember, and that the oldest of us saw for ourselves. They were once the locusts of the north, taking everything they found and killing without remorse. They openly used magic, and didn't care who saw them. They were unstoppable. Our clans, packs, and herds had no defenses against them. We couldn't find their homelands. No one knows why their attacks slowed considerably in the early 1800s, and ceased altogether by the late eighteen-eighties. It wasn't because we were winning."

The screens showed a series of sketches and illustrations of males and females wearing striking jewelry and aboriginal cold-weather gear. Some sketches were of large wolves, some with similar jewelry. A few sketches showed islands and beaches, with fins visible in the nearby water. Wolf footprints led from the shore.

"The best evidence we have is a skeleton found outside the stasis chamber that saved the Fort LeBlanc elders."

The photos showed a half-visible jawbone and skull, with huge teeth, stuck in a big pool of ice.

"This is the full skeleton, straightened out, and an artist's rendering of what it might have looked like. The bracelets and other jewelry were found as you see them."

The skeleton looked like an artist's study for a fantasy animal. The illustration looked like a salmon with legs, wearing earrings and wristbands.

Rayne felt the color drain from her face.

Triffum's words crashed into her head. "They call themselves the Ahklut. We called them Singing Death. They nearly destroyed Fort LeBlanc last time. Now they want to finish what they started. It's our job, and the job of every species that can help, to stop them."

A low thumping began reverberating through the room, as shifters began stomping their feet in agreement. War, war, *war.*

The moon goddess must hate Rayne.

In all likelihood, she'd have to kill the very people who Arvik hoped to find.

And if the moon goddess really hated her, she might have to kill Arvik, too, if he'd already found them and his current silence meant he'd chosen to join them again.

16

The huge fairy portal opened wide. The magic danced along Raynes senses, raising the hair on the back of her neck. She kept her head down and took two steps toward it.

"Chekal!"

Rayne hid a wince and turned to a thunderous Brooker. She smiled as if it had been weeks instead of hours since she last saw him.

He drilled her with his gaze. "Your name was on the roster for the second wave."

"I know. Someone, and I can't imagine who, must have made a terrible mistake, so I fixed it." She widened her smile. "Besides, you're not the boss of me, oh newly appointed Shifter Tribunal Council Special Liaison to the North American Sanctuary Cities. S-T-C-S... That's a lot of letters after your name."

He hissed his displeasure. "It's temporary."

"Good, because it's making you grumpier than usual." She waved toward the portal. "But as long as Myelle is my acting boss, she says what goes, and right now, she says

I go."

His lips twisted in annoyance. "The Council still wants to know where you got your counterintelligence about the Ahklut."

Sharing the actionable information had been the right thing to do, because even Arvik had described his former tribe as a deadly scourge.

Rayne kept her smile diamond bright. "Ghost moon wolves. I traded them for the blood of a trapper."

Guilt and regret sank sharp dire-wolf teeth into her heart with every fact she revealed, especially her theories on how to fight them.

Brooker shook his head. "You are more stubborn than your father ever was. I put you in the second wave because one of the prophecies mentions you."

"I know. Look to the North Star for Skyla." She missed Lerro's refreshingly specific pronouncements.

He shook his head. "That was one oracle. This is a prophecy. Here." He handed her a folded piece of paper. "Don't get caught."

With that cryptic warning, he turned and strode away.

She shoved it into her pocket. A prophecy was usually nothing more than a revelation of oracles writing bad poetry by committee, only comprehensible after the fact. She realigned the backpack's straps on her shoulders, then joined the ranks of armored shifter enforcers porting from the marbled hall into the outdoor world of Fort LeBlanc.

Probing magic flared, sort of like Kotoyeesinay's barrier, but less subtle. She let it see her shifter nature but fended off deeper queries. She wasn't offended that they tried. It was war, or soon would be.

The few low-resolution pictures she'd seen of the town hadn't prepared her for experiencing the amazing architecture firsthand. Trees and rocks blended as if in a symbiotic relationship to create organic buildings, some four or five stories high. Heavy-duty layered illusions hid it from the outside world of satellite imagery and wandering humans, which made it all the more fantastic.

To her left, she recognized the three majestic evergreen trees, tall as redwoods, that marked the center of town. The street beneath her boots looked like a channelized lava flow of gray quartz that reflected the hazy afternoon sunlight. Shrubs and grasses glittered without sunlight and waved without any wind. Magic was everywhere.

She marched with the fifty volunteer enforcers from prides, clans, and packs throughout the Americas. Not many had known each other until arriving in Chicago a few days ago. An alpha gray-wolf shifter with a century of special forces experience had organized them into small squads and told them to work out tactics among themselves. It had worked better than Rayne would have expected.

After a few short blocks, she stepped out and stopped at an intricately carved stone bench. A large window in front of her facing the street advertised baked goods. Swinging her backpack forward and bending to open it served as a cover for sending out her discovery magic.

Her idea had been to wait until dark, then use her skills to track down the Siberian tiger shifter named Nic. Once again, reality stomped on her plans with turf cleats.

The town was alive. Not just full of hundreds of people from dozens of species, but the town itself bordered on sentient. Far beyond a normal elven glade, where elves and the land shared strength for mutual protection.

Invisible threads connected everything, including the people she took to be citizens. More threads floated above the marching shifters as they passed by. Floated above her, too. The bristling defenses she could sense made those at the Shifter Tribunal headquarters seem quaint.

There would be no slithering through the shadows of sleepy side streets. She'd be lucky just to stay unnoticed in the makeshift barracks on the northwestern end of town.

Increasing clouds from the west and a falling temperature warned of a coming storm.

She zipped the backpack shut and slung it over her shoulder as she caught up with the rest of the shifters.

She'd been in the midst of several human wars and one shifter-clan war in Brazil, but only as a spy on covert missions, never as a soldier. Doubt and fear soured her stomach. People she didn't know and some she did would die. All the fight training in the world couldn't save them, or protect her from loss.

The barracks turned out to be fifty tents and a few food and supply trucks fitted with ice treads. The field behind them had snow tractors, snowmobiles, and a variety of military-grade Humvees. The modern equipment looked out of place in Fort LeBlanc.

A bald polar fairy in polished black armor stood on a floating chariot and bellowed at the shifters as they claimed tents.

"I am Town Elder and War Leader Rorabek. Your leaders will report to me. Gasoline vehicles are prohibited in town. Small electric vehicles are acceptable on the main roads. Do not pee on the rock giants or the trees, and do not shit in the woods—use the toilets. You have thirty minutes to stow your gear, then proceed to the southeast field, near the river, for a briefing. Don't be late, or I *will* send the forest giants after you." He pointed to one standing near the trees. She stood ten feet tall, with huge shoulders and oddly jointed hips. Long brown fur started at her feet and only stopped at her brown face. Her evil grin said she'd love to have a shifter as a fetch toy.

Rayne chose a tent on the outer edge of the encampment and dropped off her backpack on the cot in the far corner. She'd already put most of her gear in her personal magical arsenal and wardrobe, so she'd filled her backpack with extra food and entertainment. As soon as the second wave of shifters arrived, she'd be sharing the tent, but for now, it was all hers.

Before anyone realized she didn't belong to any of the squads, she shifted and nosed her way out of the tent and headed toward the town. She'd seen enough animals in Fort LeBlanc that her current borzoi illusion wouldn't cause comment.

From the map she'd memorized, the streets radiated like spokes from the center glade and park. She'd already noticed that businesses intermixed randomly with personal residences. Getting a sense of the town and searching for a half-remembered Siberian tiger's scent would be better than brooding.

She was just rounding a corner occupied by a small house, one of the few made of red brick, when she detected an unexpected familiar scent. She slowed, casting back and forth for the trail. It led back toward the center part of town, where she lost it altogether. Too many scents mingled. Too many people that might notice an excitable sighthound behaving like a stubborn bloodhound.

She took off running like she heard the dinner bell, and just barely made it to Rorabek's briefing in time. She slipped under a tree, shifted, then strolled out in her human form. She stood at the back of the crowd, near a squad of shifters she didn't know.

Rorabek was probably a volatile pain in the ass to work with closely, but she gave him credit for simple tactics that took advantage of the strengths of the shifters, elves, fairies, vampires, and magic users that would be defending the town.

"Last time, they caught us unaware. Only sleeping saved us." His chariot rose as he brandished a magical lance and raised his voice to the sky. "This time, we are awake! This time, we are ready!"

The resounding cheer echoed in her ears as she slipped away. Motivational speeches usually had the opposite effect on her. One more trait that meant she'd probably always be an outsider. She shifted again and ran back to the red-brick house.

This time, she traced the fading scent the other direction, but lost it when the compacted dirt path she'd been on came to an end in front of rough terrain and sparse evergreens.

After a long moment of listening to gusts of wind bringing snippets of sounds from the town behind her, she retraced her steps.

Back near the center of town, in human form, she bought two stuffed croissants from the bakery and sat on the stone bench out front to eat them. Savoring her prizes gave her the chance to watch and listen.

Like Kotoyeesinay, Fort LeBlanc was a United Nations of magical species, some of whom were traditional enemies in the world at large. She even saw an Arctic elf and polar fairy kiss, then realized the fairy was War Leader Rorabek.

Despite the impending trouble and the palpable tension in the air, people still took time to greet their friends. Children giggled and chased one another. Three crow shifters flew through like phantom jets, cawing loud laughter when they caused people to duck.

She couldn't trust anyone in Fort LeBlanc or Kotoyeesinay with her suspicion. Sanctuary towns usually required formal requests from outsiders to arrest citizens, or even visitors. Considering the turmoil of the impending war, the petition would take weeks or months. Plenty of time for her quarry to disappear again.

All thoughts of the hunt flew out of her head when the man she'd been hoping to find stepped out of the community center building and onto the street. Nic, the crafty tiger shifter, in the flesh and coming in her direction.

The main thoroughfare was too public for a reunion. She stood, brushed the pastry flakes off her utility vest, and sauntered up the street. Reflective surfaces told her when he passed by, and the intersection where he turned.

She looked at her watch, shook her head, then walked as if she had somewhere to be and turned at the same intersection. She kept her eyes down and matched his pace, catching and following his scent.

He slowed, looked both ways, then trotted across another street. When she glanced up, she saw him step onto the partially snow-covered ground and head toward a glade of trees.

She slowed. The glade would certainly be more private, but she could already feel its powerful magic like an Arctic breeze. On the other hand, she might never have another chance. She followed his footsteps into the glade.

Powerful probing magic washed over her, and she stopped to let it see her peaceful intentions. It let her in.

Like other glades she'd seen, it was larger than it looked from the outside, and had its own ecosystem. This one looked like a frosty twilight garden, with a frosty, crystalline floor, mossy rocks, and clusters of tiny plants everywhere.

Up ahead, Nic waved. Her knees nearly buckled when she saw who he was waving to.

Her beautiful, beloved sister, Skyla. Healthy and happy.

And mated to the big tiger, from the neon-bright bonds surrounding them like an aura. He scooped her up into a twirling embrace and kissed her soundly.

Relief and wonder flooded Rayne's chest. Her eyes ached with tears. She drew breath to call out, then froze. She was a perpetual nexus of trouble. She loved her job, but Skyla never signed up for that kind of life. What if–

"Rayne?"

Skyla's voice sounded tentative as she looked straight at her, holding out her hand. Nic stood at her side, all his attention on his mate.

Rayne nodded, not trusting her voice.

To hell with her doubts and guilt. She would take her lumps as they came. No way was she isolating herself again and hoping for the best. Squaring her shoulders, she strode across the glade.

Skyla's eyes widened. "Oh my god, you're real!"

Before Rayne could puzzle that out, she had armfuls of her baby sister. This was her pack. This was home.

Skyla squeezed Rayne tight. "Don't ever do that again! I thought you were another ghost, come to tell me how you'd died."

"What?" Rayne shook her head and drew in a deep whiff to memorize Skyla's new scent, the one that blended with Nic's.

Skyla loosened her arms and looked up at her. "The town is full of spirits. Hundreds of them, from the last time the Ahklut attacked. They told me about their deaths, and I wrote it down. The glade is their home base."

Rayne smiled. She'd never been able to see ghosts, but she knew Skyla could both see and hear them. "I'm not a spirit. Not yet, at any rate." She kissed her on the forehead. "Introduce me to your wickedly clever tiger mate."

Skyla beamed. "And wickedly sexy. He sees spirits now, too." She held out her hand.

Nic slipped his hand into Skyla's and gave Rayne a pleasant smile. "I don't know how you survived that beating, but I'm glad you made it out of the auction house alive. I'm Nic Paletin, by the way."

Skyla caught Rayne's hand. "Come home with us. We have a house here in town. We have so much to tell you."

"And I have a lot to tell you, but I have to check in with the shifter brigade commander, or they'll report me as AWOL. I do *not* want to be carried by the scruff of my neck through town by an Arctic forest giant."

Skyla popped the last bite of green tea mochi ice cream ball into her mouth. "There are some people you need to meet."

Rayne leaned back in the soft chair. "Can it wait an hour?" Her inner dire wolf groaned, temporarily mollified by the fine meal and the reunion with her only family. "I'm in a homemade-lasagna coma."

Nic chuckled as he gathered the empty bowls and plates, then headed for the open kitchen.

Rayne had confessed her transgressions against her sister, and been forgiven, even for shattering the family tracking spell. Tears had been shed, including some by a badass covert agent.

Skyla described her adventures with escaping the auction house, meeting the ghosts, mating with Nic, and defeating the wizard army. Rayne felt newly guilty that she hadn't been there to protect her sister, but relieved that she'd found Nic. They were perfect together.

"Okay, but soon." Skyla's smile faded. "The spirits are

agitated enough to brave your magic so they can warn us that time is short."

"My illusions bother ghosts?" asked Rayne.

"No, what you call your discovery magic. It's a variant of mirror and knowing magic. It's hard on them."

In addition to being a dire-wolf shifter, her brilliant sister was also a magic prodigy, and now a certified magister at an unheard-of young age.

Rayne frowned. "I'm not using it right now."

Skyla smiled. "It's who you are. If you'd ended up as a paleontologist, you'd be discovering new fossils, even if you weren't looking."

"You have a point." Paleontology had been her instant childhood obsession after their first of many visits to the La Brea Tar Pits exhibits in Los Angeles. For the first time, she and Skyla could claim their own species—*Canis dirus*—and not just be suspected of carrying a genetic defect. It still didn't explain how they both turned out to be Ice Age dire-wolf shifters with no history of wolves or mythical animals in their convoluted family trees, but the gods must have had their reasons.

Rayne yawned, then made herself get out of the sneaky nap-inducing chair to stretch. "Speaking of unexpected discoveries, do you remember Aldenrud, the auction-house manager? Corporate manager type, usually smelled like Portuguese garlic sausage and tropical-flavored nicotine?"

Skyla nodded, and Nic said he did.

"I think I smelled him here in Fort LeBlanc." She'd already given them the saga of the fall of the auction house. "It's the perfect place to hide until the heat is off. Díaz said he's got friends everywhere."

She'd walked a gray line when talking about the nebulous situation with Arvik. It was easier to continue using his undercover name.

"Fuck," said Skyla. Curses always sounded worse when she said them, because it contradicted her professorial look.

"Yeah," Rayne agreed. "Nothing we can do now, but I didn't want you to be surprised."

A tuneful chorus of bird chirping arose from the front hall.

Nic dropped the dish towel on the counter. "I'll get it."

At Rayne's perplexed look, Skyla laughed. "Doorbell."

Moments later, Nic returned, accompanied by a flame-haired man and an olive-skinned woman dressed in jeans and flannel shirts, just like Skyla and Nic. Their mate bond glowed just as bright as Skyla and Nic's, too.

Skyla laughed and stood. "I should have known you'd come." She turned to Rayne. "This is Moira and Chance. I was going to take you to meet them tomorrow. They're both *Panthera atroxes*. You'll love seeing them—eight hundred pounds each of Ice Age American lions. Moira is a mirror mage." Skyla slipped her hand into Rayne's and turned to the visitors. "This is my sister, Rayne. She came with the Shifter Tribunal contingent. She has knowing magic. She's a dire wolf, too."

Rayne appreciated her sister's discretion about her job. "It's a pleasure to meet you. Do you live here?"

Moira shook her head. "No, we're from Kotoyeesinay." Moira's easy smile lit up her face as she nudged her mate with her shoulder. "We lucked into being around for the grand reopening."

Nic tilted his head toward them. "First, they had to help defend against the wizards. They happened to hike into Fort LeBlanc two days after it reappeared."

A delicate thread of magic drifted by. If Rayne hadn't spent time with Lerro, she might not have noticed the confluence magic. "Just in time, I'm guessing."

Moira beamed. "Exactly."

"Actually," said Chance, "we saw your light on and stopped by to volunteer for school guard duty."

Nic nodded. "Raffa will be glad to have you."

Skyla squeezed Rayne's hand. "Raffa is one of the MacKenzie crows, and Nic's new business partner in a geology venture to help the town. She's an organizing queen. Last time, the Ahklut went after children especially. The teachers couldn't fight them."

Intuition bloomed in Rayne. "I heard in a briefing that the Ahklut's most powerful weapon is compelling people to listen and feel whatever the Ahklut want. Usually fear. A kind of influence magic." That's how it felt to her when Arvik had used it in the auction house, so that's what she'd told the Tribunal.

But now that she thought about, the captive shifters had listened raptly, as if bespelled. The humans hadn't noticed. She'd listened because it was Arvik. The same was true when he'd sung to the injured wolf. She'd heard and felt the call, but it was her own longing for a mate that made her want to create a pack with him.

She circled a finger to indicate all of them. "Ice Age shifters may be immune." She glanced at Nic. "Their bonded mates, too. Not even the strongest alpha magic can touch you, right? Regardless of species?"

Moira and Chance exchanged a look, then nodded.

Nic frowned. "The auction wizards put charmed pellets in all of us captives. They used a golem spell to operate my tiger like a puppet."

Skyla let go of Rayne's hand to cross to her mate to put her arm around his waist. "That's different. None of us would have been immune from that."

Rayne shook her head. "I'm not saying we won't feel fear. I'm just saying that I think the Ahklut can't *make* us feel it."

Nic put his arm around Skyla. "Okay. Then I'll definitely tell Raffa to put Moira and Chance with the kids. If they aren't scared, the kids won't be, either."

Rayne admired the hell out of Nic for accepting that his mate might be stronger than he was. Skyla deserved someone that confident in himself and her.

Chance and Moira only stayed a few minutes more, then left, with Nic showing them to the door.

"You can stay here tonight." Skyla smiled teasingly. "I'll even let you up on the couch if you don't shed too much."

Rayne chuckled. "Thanks, but I better not. The rest of the shifters will all want to come."

Skyla's look turned speculative. "What's with you and Díaz?"

Rayne might have known Skyla would pick that up. "It's complicated."

It's easy, if you'd let it be, groused her inner dire wolf.

Rayne rolled her shoulders back against the despair that tried to weigh them down. "What's your emergency station?"

"The glade. The spirits need us." Skyla wrapped Rayne in a hug better than any bear. "Don't you fucking die." She loosened her hold to catch Rayne's gaze and hold it. Tears filled her eyes. "But if you do, come find us."

"I love you, Skyla. I don't tell you often enough."

"You do." Skyla gave her a watery smile. "Just not with words."

"I'll try to be better." Rayne stepped back. "But right now, I have a job to do, and you have a mate to snuggle."

At the front door, Nic handed Rayne her coat, and Skyla handed her a slim paperback titled *Spirits*. "This might be hard to read, because it's about how the ghosts of Fort LeBlanc died, but you might learn more about the Ahklut and their tactics."

"Thanks." Rayne stuffed it into the big bellows pocket of her coat. "If any forest giants come looking for me, tell them you already sent me back to camp."

Rayne shifted and trotted straight to her tent, avoiding the impromptu squad get-togethers. She cast a small mage light and read Skyla's book. Even knowing what to expect, it made Rayne cry more than once.

It made her all the more determined to protect the people from the Ahklut. She hoped that one day, Arvik would forgive her.

17

Arvik-the-timber-wolf stayed in the middle of the pack of wolves running hard and fast across the untamed tundra. The effort kept them all focused on their magic and their feet.

In his youth, four thousand Ahklut had the strength and stamina to cover three hundred kilometers in a day, and still had energy to attack.

Times had changed.

At a hundred kilometers from their destination, most of the six hundred tribe members stumbled with fatigue. The leaders would have no choice but to stop for the night. The boggy, half-frozen terrain would be too treacherous, even with magic and moonlight to guide their way.

Moments later, the leaders sent an image to the tribe of all the wolves resting on the low, flat knoll up ahead. Few reacted when they got the news. They tiredly staggered up the incline and dropped anywhere there was room, without regard to family or clan.

Arvik was in better shape, but he lay down and panted

heavily with the rest. Nothing to see. Just another exhausted Ahklut timber wolf.

Keeping his wolf's senses alert for trouble, he sang without voice, renewing the native magic that told the rest of the timber wolves that they knew him and that he belonged with them. His experience with Rayne and the Montana gray wolves had given him the idea. So far, it had worked better than he'd hoped.

It seemed to Arvik that all the long and winding roads of his five hundred years had led him to this spot, this moment. Infiltrating his former tribe for the good of all his people. For the fervent hope of a future. A future with Rayne.

Leaving Montana and his almost-mate had been an epic battle between him and his animal spirits. They'd finally given him a few days to find his people, or port straight to Rayne, regardless of where she was.

He didn't know if it was good luck or bad that he quickly found far more than he'd ever imagined. His investigative skills and latent tribal pack connection made it comparatively easy to make contact. The rest of it rocked his world.

The rumors of a tribal schism had turned out to be true. After Arvik left the tribe in the early 1600s, as Europeans counted, the power-mad shaman Nu'untivut had declared that he'd killed Arvik for attempted assassination. Dissenters met with untimely accidents.

It took two centuries of planning, but one stormy day in the early 1800s, the pacifists vanished with nearly half the tribe. They created a hidden settlement in northern Mongolia, hoping in time to create a sanctuary town like the new ones in the Americas.

Unfortunately, peace had been hard to come by. The Ulu, as they called themselves, had few resources and no experience being good neighbors. They only ate well when in orca form. They didn't speak any other human languages besides their own. The rest of the northern peoples only saw killers. The polar fairies and the Arctic elves were on a collision course for war, and all of Siberia would be the battleground.

The breakaway Ulu colony finally abandoned Mongolia and resettled on an island west of Vancouver in 1852. They learned from their previous mistakes, and the community thrived.

It took Arvik six days to locate and make contact with the first Ulu he'd seen in four hundred years. She'd sent him to "meet some people" in Vancouver.

He'd prepared spells and his heart for every scenario he could imagine, from indifference, to suspicion, to execution. Dressed as if looking for an office job, he'd walked into the nondescript office building at the address he'd been given. When he'd ridden the elevator, he'd heard the faint undertones that meant people like him were close.

The sign on the suite's door said Qila Tours. He knocked. Before he could step back to wait, the door opened, and a politely smiling woman ushered him in. She led him to a conference room, then exited and shut the door behind her.

A wave of familiar native magic surrounded Arvik, sending a symphony of images. A silver-haired man in Western clothes, sitting at the far end of the table, stood up. He looked respectably middle-aged. "Maq'arviqeriq."

Arvik nodded, fighting with everything he had to stay calm and alert. "U'uttak." He touched two fingers to his lips, then to his chest as he sent a round of images of his own.

U'uttak looked Arvik up and down, as if sizing him up for a new suit. "You're later than we'd hoped." He shook his head. "I will never hear the end of this from your grandmother."

Arvik allowed himself a faint grin. "She has not yet kicked you out of her home, then?" In the old ways, the female owned and inherited the dwelling, and invited one or more males to live with her.

"No, but this might be the salmon that breaks the net. I didn't tell her about this meeting because I didn't want her heart to be broken again." He glanced away briefly. "We were fooled once before."

Arvik pointed a thumb toward the back door to the conference room, where he could feel the presence of three more Ulu. "Are we all meeting here, then?"

In answer, his usually non-demonstrative grandfather came around the table and wrapped him in a smothering hug. The three spirits in him twined together with the spirits of his grandfather, then pulled apart again.

His grandfather laughed. "No. Your grandmother will kill me if I don't bring you home."

Arvik stood with his back to the wall, hands in his pockets, watching five elders mingle in the living room of his grandparents' modest house. They all had public-use names, as did his grandparents, but he used their tribal names out of respect.

His brain was as stuffed as his stomach. It felt better than he could have imagined to be surrounded by family. He thought they'd been speaking English out of deference to him, since he hadn't spoken Ulu for centuries, but they'd admitted they now only used it in ceremonies. Facts, songs, history, observations, and realizations all clamored for attention. He needed time to sort them all out, but the furtive glances his direction and murmured conversations told him something was up.

At a nod from his grandfather, everyone found a place to sit. Arvik chose a stiff-backed chair from the dining room.

His grandmother, Kallulik, put her chair right next to his and sat. She carried her years with dignity, and wore stylish modern clothes and an abundance of unique jewelry. Her scent stirred memories he'd thought lost to time.

She took his hand in hers. "Tell me about this smiling brown woman and big white wolf woven into your life song." It would have been hurtful—and likely impossible—to block his beloved grandparents from seeing the images that came from his experiences. Her voice was low and confidential, but he knew everyone in the room would be listening in.

"Before I do, tell me if the Ulu can form a mate bond with a true shifter. The teaching stories I remember say the Great Singer gave us a choice of bonds or stealth, and we chose the latter."

Kallulik smiled. "I see the direction of this current. What do your *malruk* say?" The native word meant "two," but she held up three fingers to mean him and his animals.

"That she is ours, and we are hers. But she deserves the bond." It was the unique blessing of shifters that even the ancient races envied.

Kallulik patted his hand. "I will answer, but first, you are old enough to learn the truth of our origin." He felt like a human youngling, about to be told the facts about Father Christmas.

She turned to Tungamaq, the oldest male in the group. "Mack, you sing it best."

Mack nodded, then took a deep breath and let it out slowly. "Our song-keeper tales tell us the shamans of two shifter tribes, the orcas and the timber wolves, used their magic to save both from the end of the ice." Flows of familiar images accompanied his words. The ice and snow of the Ice Age retreating, wolves and orcas dying of heat, starving, hunted by encroaching humans. A circle of shamans working great magic to blend two shifter species into a single, three-spirited whole.

"When we left to settle in Siberia and embrace the way of peace, a polar fairy told us a different story. We refused to hear, at first, but time opened our ears."

New, brighter images threaded into the mix. People Arvik didn't know in lands he didn't recognize. A grievously wounded polar fairy being nursed to health. Families arguing. An angry song-keeper storming out of a council. An Ulu woman holding out her hands with magic rising from her palms.

Mack looked up. "The fairy told us the Ulu were created millennia in the past by a dark elf. A small, vengeful tribe of fairies commissioned us to be an unstoppable army to punish all who wronged them." He held up one hand with five fingers splayed, the traditional sign for a secret about to unfold.

"The dark elf has gone by many names, Surasa among them, and is known throughout this world's history for breeding monsters. The fairies asked for creatures of land and ocean, able to think for themselves and work as a unit, but controllable. Surasa captured an orca-shifter pod and a timber wolf-shifter pack, forced them to breed, then worked terrible magic on their offspring to create the Ulu. She named us the 'sharp edge,' for the weapon we were meant to be."

"The vengeful fairies mistreated our long-ago ancestors. They escaped and hid deep underwater in the frozen north. The fairies could not follow. Their enemies soon obliterated them. Ahklut was chief because he was the First Ulu and held us in sway with magic. We only knew war, and carved our name across the vast glaciers." Mack's hand dropped to his thigh, signaling the end of the tale.

Arvik let the silence settle, then ducked his head. "I am grateful for your song." Intuition danced in him. "It would explain why we're vulnerable to some fairy magic, but not all. Why we are orca but not, and why we communicate with sounds and images as well as words."

Kallulik patted his hand again. "It is good that you have an open ear, Grandson. You took pieces of our hearts when you left, but time and travel have tempered you." She leaned closer, nudging his shoulder with hers. "To answer your question, yes, bonds are rare, but possible. You must share your heart song, and your mate must hear it. Then you can get to the sexy part she will need." She squeezed his hand, then let it go.

U'uttak cleared his throat. "There is more you must know. It is our fault the sanctuary town of Fort LeBlanc was nearly destroyed."

Arvik blinked. That scenario wasn't even in his wildest dreams.

"When we left to become the peaceful Ulu, the shaman Nu'untivut told the remaining Ahklut that a few troublemakers kidnapped the rest to be their slaves. With every raid, he sent searchers looking for us, but Mongolia is vast and we hid well. When we moved here to avoid the fairy-elf war, we made new friends and alliances. Some still feared us, but we kept our spears buried and our hearts open. Then an Ahklut spy found us."

The images that accompanied his song showed the elders, including his grandparents, welcoming a tall, dark-haired man who resembled Arvik.

"We uncovered his treachery. We let him think he

escaped so we could track him." U'uttak drained the last of his glass of water.

Ukpik, a beautiful native woman with a cascading ponytail of snow-white hair, took up the tale. "We knew Nu'untivut would have to come 'rescue' us if he wanted to keep power. With reduced numbers, the Ahklut had turned to piracy, but couldn't compete with steamships. Whalers killed them as easily as thunderbirds once did. As wolves or humans, they couldn't compete against the waves of colonization."

Kallulik stood and collected empty glasses. "We attacked first."

Ukpik nodded. "A difficult choice for a peaceful people, but necessary for our survival. The Ahklut would leave a trail of blood to get to us. We captured Nu'untivut and his top warriors. With help from elf and fairy friends from Vancouver, we put them to sleep underground near Hudson Bay."

U'uttak blew out a noisy breath. "We made two mistakes. First, we assumed the remaining Ahklut would be grateful for our help."

The accompanying images showed angry Ahklut, living in stinky squalor inside rotting hand-hewn houses, spitting on the Ulu's gifts of food, and closing their ears and eyes to the Ulu songs. The last image showed the offended but saddened Ulu shifting into orca form and swimming away.

"Second," continued U'uttak, "we thought the permafrost would keep Nu'untivut frozen forever."

Arvik incongruously found himself wishing for popcorn. Wishing that Rayne was there, because she loved a good story. Wishing she was there because he needed her in his arms to calm his restless animals.

U'uttak frowned. "After only fifty years, in 1937, Nu'untivut awoke. He used his magic to free himself and his loyal warriors. The Ahklut welcomed them home, hoping for a return to the days when they could terrorize at will and eat like kings. The only Ahklut child born in the last hundred years came into her own as an oracle. Nu'untivut saw Inyiqti's value where the others had not."

Kotierik, the youngest of the elders, grimaced. "We didn't learn any of this until too late. To our shame, we ignored the Ahklut. Their rejection stung, and we believed they would fall apart without the shaman's charisma."

Arvik respectfully stayed quiet, even though he could vividly imagine where this was going.

His grandmother nodded. "Yes, Grandson, I hear your song. You guessed correctly. Nu'untivut unified the Ahklut by giving them the town of Fort LeBlanc to hate. He wanted revenge because he assumed our allies came from there. With the help of his new oracle and his own considerable magic, he and his warriors led the Ahklut in the stealth raid that slaughtered hundreds and nearly destroyed the town."

Kotierik bowed his head. "Our attack force missed the raid, but caught the Ahklut on their way back to Hudson Bay. We again captured Nu'untivut and his loyal warriors and, this time, put them and the oracle to sleep under the ice in Kalaallit Nunaat. By the time we got back to Canada, Fort LeBlanc had vanished, and the rest of the Ahklut raiders had retreated to their island."

A long moment of silence prevailed as images of the atrocities the Ahklut had perpetrated against the people of Fort LeBlanc finally faded.

One by one, everyone in the room focused on Arvik.

The puzzle pieces snapped into place. He finally understood why the elders had dropped everything to meet him. "Nu'untivut is back, and he and the Ahklut are going after Fort LeBlanc again." He sat up straight in his chair. "And you want me in the attack force."

Kallulik took his hand again, her expression grave. "No, Grandson. That is for us and our allies. Only you, with your past and magic, can do the task we ask of you." She took a deep breath. "Become one of them. Weaken them from the inside."

Arvik wanted nothing more than to port himself and Rayne to a paradise island and dance with her as long as it took to become her mate. But he still owed atonement. He couldn't leave the rest of the world vulnerable to a vicious predator like Nu'untivut. Not when he could help.

He took a deep breath and let it out slowly. "I will do it."

For the next three weeks, he'd immersed himself in the knowledge the Ulu had collected about the Ahklut. His mission and existence were kept secret from all but a few.

He missed Rayne every waking moment and in his dreams. He read all the messages from her three and four times and wished he could send more than light banter in return. He couldn't even tell her he was about to go off the grid, for fear that the Ahklut's oracle would pick up on it.

Minutes before he was about to port himself to the eastern shore of Hudson Bay, he handed his grandmother a note. "If I am lost, please contact the Shifter Tribunal in Chicago with this message."

"I will." Kallulik hugged him tightly, then whispered in his ear. "Find out if she has a nice house."

The snow melted under Arvik's belly, dampening his fur and chilling him to the bone. He'd lost his tolerance for the bitter cold. Ordinary Ahklut wolves didn't need to use magic to stay warm in late fall, so he couldn't, either.

The last three weeks with his former tribe had been a

harsh reminder of how he had once been, and how far he'd come since.

The Ahklut had once thrived on three hidden islands in the Arctic, but were now barely surviving on the smallest. Their collective magic had weakened as they lost tribe members, so it was all they could do to maintain the communal spells that hid them. Healing magic had been forgotten, and it showed in the twisted limbs and scars in their various forms.

Their cabins had collapsed and been scrubbed away by a relentless succession of howling winters. The caves where they now lived were littered with older technology they couldn't use. They'd have starved long ago if they hadn't been tough-to-kill shifters who could survive on fish all year.

Arvik moved into an abandoned cave on the windward side of the island and made it his own. To others, he was a silent, morose Ahklut named Niglaktok who had no living family and only spoke when prodded. Like most of the local Ahklut, Niglaktok was down to one small adornment, a black-with-tarnish silver earring that pierced his ear cartilage. Thanks to a fairy illusion forged into the earring, the others saw an older, gaunt male with a permanently twisted back and a scarred face in human form, and an equally skinny timber wolf.

His first order of business was to use charisma magic as he made contact with other long-time residents. Only a few seemed familiar from centuries ago; he doubted they'd remember him at all. His magic made them drop their guard and forget to block their songs from untrusted strangers. He "accidentally" shared a few invented songs with them. One of being caught in an ice floe and nearly dying, others depicting lonely hunts in the deep ocean, gnawing on carrion, and avoiding humans on snowmobiles.

He borrowed melodies from the Ahklut to weave more songs to enrich his Niglaktok persona.

It helped that tiny family units sometimes didn't see anyone else for years, even if they were only separated by three or four kilometers. Hard-scrabble living left little energy for anything besides avoiding starvation and staying out of the elements.

From magical snooping, he learned that Nu'untivut and his warriors had returned to the island only about six months before. The shaman had been using his powerful magic to waylay ocean-going ships during storms so the Ahklut could steal their contents, which they'd traded or sold for food and modern weapons.

Most of the Ahklut that Arvik encountered were optimistic that the shaman would lead them to prosperity. Already, they had fresh canned meat stocked in their larders, fuel for lanterns, and new boots.

Arvik spent the rest of his time learning the local patois of English mixed with old French and older Ulu dialect, and collecting intelligence.

Nu'untivut lived in the large cave that had once served as a community hall, now lit and heated with the power of the first working generator on the island in forty years. Ten of his seventeen warriors, males and females, and the oracle, Inyiqti, who had become his lover, slept in the hall. The other seven had invited themselves as permanent guests in the closer, more comfortable caves of the locals. The one vocal protester had met with a fatal accident while on a piracy raid.

Four weeks ago, just before Arvik had arrived on the island, Nu'untivut called a gathering of all Ahklut and proposed a bold plan. His oracle had discovered their old enemy, the cowardly aggressors of Fort LeBlanc, were awake once more. Inyiqti's song had shown them a wondrous paradise city with tall buildings for houses and trees for firewood. More important, her visions showed the town sat on a rich vein of valuable raw gems, ripe for mining.

The shaman proposed that the Ahklut would take the town again. This time, as justice for the original unprovoked attack, they would keep it. The inland location would be far from the sea, but with the rich plunder of the town at their disposal, the Ahklut could afford to buy planes and fly themselves to any ocean in the world.

Arvik showed up for all the subsequent gatherings. Nu'untivut and his warriors looked proudly healthy and well-fed. Their open tunics and rolled pants showed off the full complement of tribal jewelry on ankles, wrists, arms, necks, and ears. Shining examples of what the Ahklut could be again. The shaman's songs about the coming glory were as compelling as the charisma magic he used to make the Ahklut listen and want what he was selling.

Arvik might not have recognized the magic if he hadn't already been using it for his own purposes. If his life had taken a different path centuries ago, his free magic might have made him a respected shaman instead of an outcast and a spy. But then, he wouldn't have seen the rest of the world or met Rayne, so the shaman's life had no appeal.

Even without magic, Nu'untivut was a charismatic, wily schemer with the political instincts of a grifter. Shorter than Arvik in real life, but more heavily muscled. Not handsome, but strong featured and quick to smile. He wore a mix of traditional tribal tunics and modern jeans and boot. He embraced new technology and saw its potential. With magic, he was an unstoppable monster with nine lives, and he'd only used three of them.

Arvik stayed well away from him and his raven-haired lover, Inyiqti.

In the gatherings, Arvik hunched in the back of the crowd, shielding his magic, wishing he'd learned Rayne's trick for masking her scent. Wishing she was there, to have his back. He'd operated solo for centuries, but in one short week, she'd made him want to never work alone again. Never *be* alone again.

It wasn't as easy to stay away from Nu'untivut's warriors. Their assigned task was to toughen up the locals and remind them how to work group magic and how to fight as an army. All would be needed for success, even Arvik-as-Niglaktok, once he proved his human deformity didn't carry over to his timber wolf form.

The warriors had done as well as they could with the locals, but better meals and only four weeks of training couldn't make up for decades of destitution. They could barely maintain the effort for the stealth shield that hid their approach from eyes, ears, and magic.

Now the exhausted local Ahklut lay nearly comatose on the cold, wet tundra, too tired even to sing of the Fort LeBlanc riches that would soon be theirs.

The warriors prowled, restless and agitated, noses working overtime. The shaman and four of the warriors shifted to human to talk. The other warriors stayed as wolves, but drifted closer, ears pointed toward the group.

Arvik dared a tiny tendril of native magic, asking the wind to bring him their words.

"...it's what we're *not* smelling," said one of the warriors. "No weather. No rabbits."

Another piped up. "No distant sounds, either. Just wolves and the noisy water. Why isn't it frozen?"

Arvik snorted to himself. *Welcome to climate change.*

The oracle finished shifting to human and sidled up next to Nu'untivut. "I see nothing but the river we follow that will take us to Fort LeBlanc."

Without warning, detection magic exploded from Nu'untivut like a shockwave. Every bit of active magic glowed in response as the wave passed by.

Arvik shielded, but not fast enough to stifle the brief, flare-bright glow of his multiple magics.

"Bring me that wolf," commanded Nu'untivut.

Arvik doused all his own magic, except the block that prevented nosey Ahklut from listening to his songs without asking. He pretended sleepy confusion when forcibly lifted to his feet and ordered to shift to human. He took his time doing so.

The warriors force-marched him to face the shaman and the oracle.

"Who are you?" demanded Nu'untivut.

Arvik displayed surprise that the shaman needed to ask. "I am called Niglaktok."

Inyiqti's frosty eyes squinted. "Truth, but clouded."

Nu'untivut frowned and exerted charisma pressure to be talkative, to want to please.

Sad, silent Niglaktok was too exhausted to care what the shaman thought of him. Arvik let slip a song image of discovering and mourning a dead Ahklut in orca form.

Another wave of detection magic engulfed Arvik.

Nu'untivut held out his hand. "Give me your ear cuff."

One warrior gasped, and several twitched. Even the sky-eyed oracle gave Nu'untivut a sidelong glance. Nearby local wolves raised their heads.

Niglaktok stared in mouth-agape shock.

The shaman frowned and removed a wide, beautifully decorated gold-and-silver wrist cuff and held it out toward Niglaktok. "I offer trade."

Niglaktok twisted his shoulder away and cupped his earring protectively. "No. Your *suluk* carries no heart song." *Your adornment has no memories of my family.*

Nu'untivut put the cuff back on his arm. "Enough. He's sabotaging our stealth. Even the children of Fort LeBlanc will feel us coming." He turned to the warrior to his left. "Parktoq, challenge and kill him." By tribal law, no chief or shaman could initiate a death challenge. Undoubtedly why so many of Nu'untivut's enemies had died in conveniently fatal accidents.

"No," said Inyiqti, her voice harsh, her pale eyes unfocused. "If he dies, we die." She touched her forehead. "I have seen it."

Arvik hid a frown. Lerro had said the same thing, back in the underground auction house. It was rarely good to feature in oracle visions.

Nu'untivut waved a hand impatiently. "Stake him to the ground and break his leg. We will come back for him after we take our prize." He sent a questioning glance at the oracle. She nodded.

Parktoq grabbed Arvik's arm and marched him through the resting wolves toward the outer perimeter.

Pain was nothing to an Ahklut, but tribal tradition was everything. Arvik loosed multiple songs that showed the events that had just occurred. Underneath, he compelled the local wolves to listen.

Two wolves shifted to human and moved to block Parktoq's progress. One stood with fists on his hips and tilted his head toward the shaman. "Where is the evidence? The elders were not consulted for judgment."

A grizzled older wolf stood as human and joined her tribe members. Her iron-gray hair fell in two braids down her back. Tiri glared at Parktoq, brandishing her family ring by raising her bony fist. "Whose *suluk* will you steal next?"

More wolves awoke. Some growled. Some climbed to their feet, despite their exhaustion.

Parktoq glanced back toward the shaman, but he was

walking away in the opposite direction, talking to the other warriors. "Nobody wants your..." He checked his words, but he wasn't as fast at hiding his song. Arvik made sure all the wolves saw his sneering disdain for their family adornments.

Parktoq hauled Arvik along for a few more steps. "This one is trouble."

Another man, Uklaq, stepped forward. As tall as the warrior, but older and thinner. "We are Ahklut. We are all trouble."

Parktoq's fist crashed into Uklaq's face. "Move."

Uklaq stumbled sideways, but recovered.

Tiri's power punch took Parktoq by surprise, stunning his diaphragm, causing him to let go of Arvik's arm.

A warrior in wolf form lunged toward Tiri, but Uklaq shoved it aside with his knee.

Arvik was gratified that the seeds he'd been sowing for weeks were bearing fruit, but it was too soon. He hastily shared songs of a rich city with gold streets and fantasy buildings of silver and green. With his charisma magic, he sent the soothing sensation of dream sleep.

The nearest Ahklut relaxed, entranced by the vision and their own imaginations. Arvik slouched even more and assumed a dazed look.

Parktoq shook his head as if bothered by a cloud of gnats, causing his bejeweled braids to rattle. He glared suspiciously at Arvik, then at the shaman, who had turned to look at them.

Snarling, Parktoq glared at the locals. "Down." Once they complied, he grabbed Arvik's shoulder and threw him to the ground. "Stay down and stay quiet."

Arvik shifted to wolf form even more slowly than before, then curled up as if cold and tired. Both were truer than he cared to admit.

Parktoq stomped away toward the shaman. After a long moment, the other wolf warriors slunk away, some with Parktoq and some toward the edge of the resting wolves to patrol.

Arvik tuned wolf ears and wind magic to hear Parktoq's words to the shaman.

"...stake him, the scent of blood will break our stealth. I figured it's better to bring him than leave him to talk about where we're going. If he's whole, no one has to carry him."

Nu'untivut grunted. "What upset the others?"

Parktoq made a rude noise. "They thought you wanted their *suluk*."

A gust of wind blew apart Nu'untivut's reply.

"That's what I thought. Qingak and I will keep strings on him."

Parktoq strode away.

Morose Niglaktok wouldn't think to acknowledge the Ahklut who had come to his aid, but Arvik could send a low-power wizard spell of healing to Uklaq and Tiri. They would both need strength for the upcoming run.

As much as he wanted to stay awake all night, he couldn't chance using that much magic. Supernaturally fast travel across the rough tundra took a lot of energy. Even the phenomenally powerful shaman would need to sleep before the upcoming invasion.

Arvik awoke just before dawn, chilled to the bone, but glad to be free of blood-soaked nightmares of wars gone by. His inner beasts hated unnecessary killing, and war fell into that category. He hated killing, period.

Within minutes, the warriors were up and nudging the Ahklut up onto their feet.

Traveling across the tundra like a force of nature brought back more memories of the earliest days, when he'd reveled in the strength of the pack, the thrill of victory, the glory of being alive. It took on new meaning, now that he knew their true origin. They'd been the hellfrogs of their day. But unlike those monsters, the Ahklut had free will.

The pale sun neared its high point when Nu'untivut sent images of the town's barrier, coming up soon. He and his warriors would slice it open so the rest of the tribe could blitz through the town and head straight for the glade heart. This time, the town elders could not hide. Charisma magic accompanied the images, giving the Ahklut a taste of triumph and a sense of righteous, long overdue justice.

The shaman and the warriors surged forward. Only the oracle, Inyiqti, and the warrior Parktoq stayed with the main pack.

It was now or never. Arvik slowed until he ended up in the rear of the pack. The edge of the barrier magic jarred his senses as much as the uneven ground beneath his feet. Up ahead, the magic of Fort LeBlanc already felt like a warm breeze.

One wolf at a time, he began sending nearly transparent images and quiet songs of a fork in the path. West, away from the river, led to the old familiar ways of terrible, violent victories, but also to destruction and loss. To absent leaders who took the best of everything, leaving the rest of the tribe to squabble over scraps. South led to a different life, with new friends and community, and peace. More than just clinging like a barnacle to an ice-covered rock. Neither path would be easy, but turning west meant even fewer Ahklut would see another season, and a world of enemies would be baying for their blood. Turning south with the river was a venture into an uneasy, unknown future in a modern world they'd only seen the edges of, but at least they'd *have* a future.

Arvik ran a weaving path that moved him forward in the pack, sharing the song with each Ahklut he passed. The shared shield magic would have made an instant conduit, but he couldn't afford for his images to be seen by the wrong wolves.

Nu'untivut sent a strong image to the tribe to circle left to avoid a forest area of aged pines that would slow them down. The new direction put them closer to the river, and closer together.

Arvik took a chance and sent his message to multiple wolves as he passed them, edging toward the front. They were getting nearer to the decision point, and he still needed to sing to another hundred wolves.

18

Rayne trotted westward on four feet, just below the snowy ridge, sniffing the air, listening past the wind. Her position gave her the full view of the tiny round valley just north of Fort LeBlanc. A long-ago glacier had gouged the broken-bowl shape. At the rim, wind-blown snow decorated the leftover boulders and the scraggly trees that had grown around them.

Three full days of patrol and more hours that morning reminded her how much she hated stakeouts. At least she wasn't stuck in some smelly van, eating junk food and peeing on puppy pads. The sun had passed its anemic zenith an hour ago, and she still had no clue if they were in the right place or wasting time.

It was all Brooker's fault. When she'd gone back to the shifter tents after the comforting evening with Skyla and her mate, she'd finally remembered the prophecy Brooker had handed her. She'd been ready to ignore it, but her discovery magic sent chills down her spine as she read the note.

Black and white wolves

take the high ground in timber gray.
Luck and Destiny drive trouble north;
Tears from the Sky and her Bowhead
must become trouble to stop it.
Only the wings of thunder can end it.

It was much more specific than the usual vague poetic language salad. Maybe Lerro had shown up to help them.

She'd gone back to Skyla and Nic's house that night. They'd asked Moira and Chance to return and called other trusted friends, and come up with a plan.

Everyone agreed the prophecy called for her and Skyla to be on the high ground—only the northern ridge fit the bill—and wearing the illusions of timber wolves. They were pretty sure Luck and Destiny meant Chance and Moira, whose huge American lions could scare the shit out of modern shifters, just like dire wolves could.

The rest of their strategy rested on a shakier foundation of inspiration and guesswork. Rayne would have preferred basing it on actual facts instead of a prediction, but she'd learned to trust her own magic. Moira had disbelieved in magic until a few months ago. She was less certain of her intuition, but damn good with mirrors.

They'd tried to take their ideas to the town defenders, but Rorabek, the polar fairy war leader, and the other Fort LeBlanc elders had no time for them. Both Rayne and Moira agreed the elders were hiding something big, but neither wanted to risk exposing it for their own curiosity.

Last night had brought strange and troubling dreams of wars she'd never seen. It had taken an hour of pacing in the chilly darkness to clear her head.

For reasons she couldn't name, she'd been increasingly tense all morning. Even though the town was a few miles south, Fort LeBlanc's defensive magics rubbed her fur the wrong way. She felt like she'd dragged Skyla into another dangerous situation, even though her sister had insisted on coming.

Rayne followed Skyla's scent to the cluster of trees at the western edge of the bowl. They shifted to human and hunkered down together so they wouldn't have to compete with the noisy wind.

"You yipped?" asked Rayne.

"Something's coming." Skyla pointed east. "It's like a mass of nothing moving toward us as fast as a convoy of trucks, but there aren't any roads that direction."

Rayne opened her collar to free one of the comms necklaces she'd borrowed from the Shifter Tribunal and handed out to their team. "How big, and how far away?"

"Smaller than a caribou herd, but not by much. Maybe fifteen miles. I'll try a scrying spell when they get closer." Skyla shook her head. "I don't know how you do this for a living, waiting for stuff to happen. Makes me want to pee on every bush, so I won't have a full bladder when I have to run."

Rayne nudged her sister's knee with hers. "This is the anti-fun part. I've wanted to wet a few shrubs myself." She activated the comms device and spoke into it. "Skyla's magic says a cloaked mass is coming from the east. Showtime in thirty minutes." The team all had the same comms devices and would hear, regardless of form.

After dropping the necklace back inside her coat, she gave her sister a brief hug. "*Canis dirus, unum.*"

Skyla smiled. "We should add 'Panthera atrox' and the others to our call to arms."

Rayne laughed. "Might be a little unwieldy. Maybe we should just say 'Ice Age shifters unite.' Nic can be honorary." She pointed east. "I'm going back to the east edge, in case any ghosts want to talk to you."

Skyla nodded, then shifted into wolf form as fast as an

eyeblink. She had improved the spells that made them both look like ordinary gray wolves, but Rayne knew her scent anywhere.

Rayne shifted in seconds, touched muzzles with Skyla, then took off across the ridge to the east.

A shockwave from attack magic exploded across her senses. The southern sky flashed brighter.

The wait was over.

Rayne ran to the vantage point she'd selected, wishing it was high enough to see Fort LeBlanc. A second shockwave from the unfamiliar attack magic blew past, like being in a momentary sandstorm. She ignored the urge to shake her fur.

The comms device beeped with Moira's tone. *"My mirror shows a big mass of heat distortion coming from the east. It's splitting in two. Part is heading south, and part is headed west toward the river."*

A third shockwave of attack magic, more powerful than before, howled through the trees and surged white noise through the comms device.

"...staying straight, but the west section is starting to cross the river. The undines won't like that. They take their river domain seriously."

Rayne shifted to human and thumbed the comms device. Before she could speak, Moira's voice continued.

"The westbound heat wave is timber wolves, maybe two hundred of them. They run fast! The undine attack uncloaked them. Holy shit, a wolf just shifted into a killer whale and ate two undines, then shifted back."

Rayne interrupted. "Moira, shift. If they go northeast, you and your badass mate have to drive them to us."

"Okay. The southern group uncloaked, too. It's more timber wolves than the west group. And there's another pack of mixed wolves running north right at them, maybe two miles away."

Rayne heard feline growling in the background. *"Okay, okay, you big furry lug. I'm shifting."*

Rayne had been near war zones before, but magical war zones were the worst. The ethereal plane vibrated with the constant drums of magical attacks and counterattacks. No shield spells that she knew would silence it.

Rayne tried to shift back, but her inner wolf refused. *Listen!*

She took a deep breath and let it out slowly. Natural wind and gusts of battlefield energy rustled the shrubs. She breathed again, trying to ignore the pressure to plan, to move, to act. She'd give it one more... A spark of warmth ignited in her chest, and blossomed through her magic.

Arvik Inuktan was near, and to the south.

She didn't want to believe he was one of the attacking Ahklut, but he hadn't been there until the cloaking shields came down. She wanted him to be one of the good myths of the world.

She shifted to wolf. The spark in her chest stayed warm and grew brighter. He was coming her way. Goddess, but she had missed him.

Long minutes later, deep feline threat yowls arose from the far rocks that Chance and Moira had staked out as theirs. An elven charm and the hard, stone surfaces made them sound like a hundred giant pissed-off lions, ready to kill anyone, and gnaw on their bones afterward.

The spark in her chest suddenly felt like a space heater. She hoped it meant the Ahklut had triggered her trap.

Everything in her wanted to run toward her mate. She tamped it down and made herself sit. The runners would have to bunch up to get past the sides of the broken bowl and into the lower valley.

Skyla's tone and voice sounded from the comms device. *"Per my scrying spell, the Fort LeBlanc defender forces have most of the western attack group jammed up against the barrier. About thirty Ahklut avoided both ambushes early and headed northeast. One of them has enough magic to sink a battleship. When Moira and Chance did their thing, the Ahklut veered north like you wanted and went through the fairy ring. We'll see them soon."*

Rayne grunted twice softly in response. Skyla would already be back in wolf form before Rayne could warn her not to take chances like that, even though the news was useful.

She'd been afraid of having to deal with a hundred or more Ahklut, but thirty was bad enough. Once they realized there was no way out, they'd be dangerous, cornered rats, led by a powerful shaman.

She hoped it wasn't Arvik. She didn't want to have to put him on her kill list. Again.

Faster than she'd imagined, a streak of running timber wolves burst through the cluster of trees and into the untouched field of snow.

The four timber wolves that led the way slowed, then angled west toward a pair of boulders. A fifth followed. The rest of the timber wolves poured into the basin and fanned out in small groups. They looked like a special-forces commando team securing a location. It would only take them minutes to realize there was no passage out of the valley.

Skyla gave a stuttering timber wolf howl, loud enough to be heard throughout the valley. Every wolf turned to look. Using her magic, she made the next howl seem like an answer from miles away.

That was Rayne's cue. She ran as fast as she dared down the slope through the cover of the trees. The charm she carried hid her from sight, but wouldn't hide her trail.

Her feet wanted to take her straight to Arvik, even though she couldn't see him yet. *Stick with the plan.*

She froze when four timber wolves appeared in between the trees to her right.

Three lanky wolves, two males and a female, stank of fear and exhaustion. The fourth, larger and heavier, stank of frustration as she slashed bites at the haunches of the others, evidently trying to hurry them.

The smallest of the wolves spun unexpectedly fast and bit her tormenter on the shoulder, hard enough to draw blood. When the large wolf snarled and launched an attack, the other two wolves threw themselves into the fray, going after the larger wolf.

The flurry of bites and lunges went on for tense seconds before the large wolf grabbed the smallest wolf by the neck and threw her up and out, sailing into a tree only four feet from where Rayne stood. The small wolf didn't move.

The other wolves pulled back from the fight, exhibiting the wolf equivalent of appeasing apology. The large, angry wolf snarled at them both, glanced toward the defeated small wolf, then stalked up the slope. The others followed more slowly, heads and tails drooping in defeat.

It was the perfect opportunity for Rayne to insinuate herself into the pack and become trouble, like the prophecy said, but she couldn't just kill the small Ahklut female to do it. Sending a prayer to the Goddess that she was doing the right thing, she shifted into human.

She spit the fairy charm out of her mouth, then cast a wizard's healing spell on the fallen wolf. She waited until the shattered shoulder finished reshaping itself before bending down to whisper in the wolf's ear. "You have choice. Give up the Ahklut way and live, or die here." She repeated the offer in French, just in case.

The wolf whined softly, then shifted into a small, wiry woman with gray braids, dressed in ancient leather and fur clothing and brand-new pink snow boots. She looked up at Rayne. Her eyes widened. "I know you. *Hilaluktoq.*"

What the hell? "Of course you do," said Rayne confidently. One did not turn away Goddess gifts, however strange. "New plan. Why don't we go meet the oth–"

A branch cracked up the slope. A magic detection spell crashed over them like a freight train, coming from the center of the valley.

Rayne shoved the suddenly glowing illusion charm into her pocket and shifted. The woman nodded, then shifted herself.

Moments later, the three wolves from above trotted into view.

Rayne mimicked the others and dropped her head and tail as she sidled closer to the smallest wolf.

The large, surly wolf issued what felt like a wordless command. Not dominance, like modern alphas sometimes tried on her. More like orders from a drill instructor. She got the vague image of wolves marching downhill.

Sure enough, the surly wolf headed off down the slope. The other wolves fell in line behind her, exhaustion dragging their feet. Rayne took up the rear, dragging her feet, too, but staying as close as possible to her new best friend.

Once they got to the lower basin, she got her first close look at more of the Ahklut wolves. Most looked even worse than her new friend, like they'd starved all winter and would topple at the slightest breeze. A few, like the surly wolf, looked well-fed and healthy, and ready for a fight.

In the center of the snowy meadow stood a heavily muscled timber wolf with a distinctive tail that look like he'd dipped it in white paint. He flaunted his magic like a peacock in rut. Next to him stood a smaller but equally healthy female. Her startling eyes were the pale blue of an aging iceberg. She didn't exude magic, but she made Rayne instantly uneasy.

The compass in her heart told her Arvik was moving, up and to the west, not anywhere close to the preening shaman.

She stifled the relief that threatened to buckle her legs. Arvik might still have embraced the Ahklut way. Not to mention, she was now playing chicken with a pack of starving timber wolves.

Another wordless command passed by her, this time from the shaman. A hazy image accompanied the command, of the narrow pass that led to the valley. Moments later, four of the healthy wolves took off at a run due south, toward the pass. None of the skinny wolves moved. Interesting mode of communication.

Her best friend sat, so she did, too.

Arvik was moving closer.

She tried to keep herself from turning to look that direction, but couldn't.

Five wolves came from behind the largest of the valley's boulders. One vigorous and energetic, four skinny and tired.

She didn't recognize any of them.

Realization penetrated her shock. He was undercover, just like she was. Again.

The gods must be laughing themselves silly.

19

Arvik-as-wolf wasn't usually bothered by complexities, but the unexpected presence of his mate sent him in twisting spirals of joy and worry. He'd sensed her the moment Nu'untivut had broken off clouding the ethereal plane with his pounding magical assaults on the Fort LeBlanc defenses. Arvik hadn't expected Rayne to be there, but he should have. If half the magical world was about to be drawn into a war, where else would she be?

When the shaman and the oracle, Inyiqti, raced north, Arvik followed, pretending blind loyalty. Five warriors and about twenty other Ahklut abandoned the attacking force and followed the shaman. He didn't know why the others did, but his goal was simple. Stop Nu'untivut.

An unearthly growling from rising rocks to the northeast sent them all veering straight north. Ahklut didn't scare easily, but no one wanted to tangle with whatever made that noise. North looked promising as far as defensible high ground. Oddly, the terrain changed, and suddenly, they were speeding up a slope and Rayne was much closer than before.

At the narrow mouth of the wide valley, Nu'untivut sent images with orders to team up, one warrior and multiple Ahklut each, to check out the area and report back.

Arvik deliberately went with the warrior Parktoq because he was headed west, away from the lodestone presence that was Rayne. Once he heard the timber wolf howl from above, he had no doubt she and the other shifters had a plan.

Nu'untivut had been forced to improvise a new battle plan after he'd failed to smash Fort LeBlanc's outer barrier. Swarming it with the combined group magic of the Ahklut might have won the day in the nineteenth century, before the invention of modern magic and military ordnance. And before he lost two-thirds of his attack force to the choice of going south.

Arvik had wanted to go with them, but he had to trust that his grandparents and the rest of the Ulu would receive them with respect and kindness. His job wasn't done.

The first of the westbound attack force had thrown themselves and their magic against the barrier. Nu'untivut's simultaneous punch had caused the earth to crack open, but not the barrier.

Arvik had been angling to get closer to Nu'untivut, when he saw Inyiqti in human form pull the shaman aside to speak urgently into his ear. Moments later, the main Ahklut force had received a flurry of images that ordered them to keep attacking with magic and physical force. Even as the last image circulated, the shaman and the oracle, once again a wolf, had run northeast.

Arvik had followed, confused, until he saw the arrival of Fort LeBlanc's defending armies attacking from two sides. Inyiqti must have seen them coming and told Nu'untivut. The shaman was jumping ship, using the frenzied Ahklut attack to cover his escape. How very like him to deem everyone but himself and a few warriors expendable.

In the valley, Nu'untivut had projected confidence, but Arvik had heard the undertone of anger and fear in his orders. Especially when his warriors began reporting the valley had no way out.

The warrior Parktoq led his group, the one Arvik-as-Niglaktok had joined, back through the big rocks and toward the wolves clustered in the center of the valley. Nu'untivut and Inyiqti stood in the center, protected by the rest of the wolves. Parktoq added his bad-news melody to the group song.

Arvik could hardly listen to anything but the siren song of his mate, who had somehow snuck into the group. He only knew which timber wolf she was because his heart told him, not because she looked different. Even Tiri, the elder Ahklut who Rayne sat right next to, accepted Rayne as one of their own. Her skill amazed him even as fear for her iced his veins.

Nu'untivut gave the order to go back the way they'd come, where he'd already sent four warriors to scout ahead. The two remaining warriors, Parktoq and Kajuq, started trotting south. The shaman and the oracle followed.

None of the other Ahklut who had followed them to the valley moved.

It took Nu'untivut a few seconds to notice. He snapped a bite at the flank of a standing wolf, who yelped and dodged, but moved north instead of heading south. Growling low and long, Nu'untivut stopped to turn and send an angry, imperative song that the valley felt like a trap. The accompanying charisma magic pushed them to fear his punishment for disobedience.

To Arvik's astonishment, three Ahklut shifted into human form. Tiri, Uklaq, and an ancient wolf Arvik didn't know moved to stand together, north of the shaman. They all stared at Nu'untivut.

After a long, tense stillness, Nu'untivut shifted into human, demonstrating his shifting speed as a show of power. He wore a mountaineer's many-pocketed parka over his deerskin shirt and military-style trek boots.

Arvik-the-wolf suppressed a disdainful sneeze. He was faster, and Rayne made them both look like snail shifters.

Nu'untivut gestured impatiently at all three. "Speak."

Tiri stepped forward. "You lost the vote. We no longer listen to your song, Nu'untivut."

"Vote?" His sneering song declared that true Ahklut didn't vote, they fought and took. "You are the ones who lost."

He turned his back on them and stalked away, his back and arms stiff, anger etched on his face.

All the other standing Ahklut sat. Except for Inyiqti. And Rayne.

Belatedly, Arvik realized he should have sat when the others did. Rayne's unwavering gaze and her unshielded song told him she was standing to support him. Warmth expanded in his heart.

Nu'untivut spun to face the elders, his expression enraged. "Who won this vote? Who will lead when the Fort LeBlanc traitors hunt you down like vermin?"

The elders turned their gaze to Arvik. The rest of the Ahklut did the same.

Just like the wolves in Montana.

Shit.

"You." Nu'untivut's expression morphed from stunned disbelief to savage aggression. "Since I'm no longer *isuraqtujuq*, I can kill you myself."

Nu'untivut's magical attack was swift, with the explosive power of a bottled storm.

The blow bounced off Arvik's shields. He shifted to human in the space of a few seconds, the fastest he'd ever done it. Magic was best worked in human form.

The oracle Inyiqti shifted to human.

Nu'untivut stomped closer, bringing down his fist, mimicking the force he lowered on Arvik.

Arvik felt it, but his shields held. He caught and held Nu'untivut's gaze and sent an image of the shaman walking away with Inyiqti and his few remaining warriors. "Your time is done."

Nu'untivut held his hand to the sky, drawing power from the clouds.

Arvik almost missed the shaman's flicked side glance. He hastily cast a firefly spell toward Nu'untivut and ran toward the trio of elders.

The witch's spell did its job, breaking the shaman's concentration for crucial seconds.

Arvik extended his shield just in time to deflect the lightning bolt and redirect it to scorch the ground a meter in front of Nu'untivut's feet. The shaman jumped back, bumping into Inyiqti.

Arvik stilled his face as he gathered the potential for all the magics he knew. "Your choices are peace, exile, or challenge. Go after anyone else, and I'll kill you where you stand."

The shaman barked a derisive laugh. "I make my own choices."

Charisma magic deluged Arvik's world. His shields were useless against the black despair that accompanied image after image of death and destruction. Peace was a myth. Arvik and every other Ahklut would be torn limb from limb by the vengeful Fort LeBlanc populace. Their stripped and broken bones would lie at the bottom of the deepest, darkest sea.

Arvik gritted his teeth and fought the onslaught with images of the wonders he'd seen in the outer world. The promise of spring and new life. The camaraderie of trusted friends. The noisy delight of children. The quiet comfort of beloved family.

Nu'untivut's river became a flood, trying to take over his will to fight, to think, to live.

Arvik reached for the only warmth he had left. Rayne.

Songs burst from the core of him. Brilliant, sexy black woman. Clever, strong white dire wolf. Adventure. Laughter. Passion. The shaman's dark magic couldn't fill a heart that was already full.

Everything in Arvik sang for the woman he loved. He hoped she could hear him.

Rayne watched the shaman showdown between Nu'untivut and Arvik. She hated feeling powerless. Meddling in magic she didn't understand got people killed. Calling in the cavalry got people killed. Breaking cover got her killed. Not protecting Arvik got *him* killed.

Tearing her attention away from the confrontation, she assessed the rest of the Ahklut. The skinny wolves just watched. The smaller female wolf with Nu'untivut shifted into a stocky-bodied, plain-faced native woman who had the same startling pale blue eyes that made her look blind. Like the asshole shaman, she wore a mix of modern and old-style clothes, and a whole shopping channel's worth of jewelry. She looked angry and scared. Rayne knew the feelings.

There was no sign of the four wolves that had gone toward the valley entrance, but the surly female and dark-furred male were stalking Arvik like he was a wounded deer.

She launched herself toward them. Sitting Ahklut scrambled out of her way.

The closer of the two stalkers turned to face her, snarling. His magic attack tried to paralyze her with fear. She went straight for his throat.

He twisted away, but she still got a mouthful of fur and a taste of blood. She lunged and bit again as he turned, this time tearing a solid chunk out of his shoulder.

His pained yelp drew the attention of the female stalker, who darted in with slashing teeth aimed at Rayne's vulnerable flank.

Dodging, Rayne used her powerful shoulders to redirect the female's momentum into the bloody male. While they stumbled together, she got ahold of a flailing back leg and bit down hard.

Not much could stand against the jaw strength of a pissed-off dire wolf. The wolf's leg crunched in her mouth like chicken bones. She shook it for good measure before she let go, making sure the leg would be unusable for a while.

The bloody male leaped on top of her, raking her ribs with unnatural, cat-like claws and biting the extra-thick fur on the back of her neck.

She bucked him off like a bronco rider, then spun and lunged into him, barreling him into the dirty snow.

The injured female squirmed toward Rayne with snapping jaws, projecting the same fear magic the male used.

Rayne channeled angry dire wolf into her warning growl at both attackers, and readied fireball spells she could cast even while in wolf form. *Do not fuck with me or my mate.*

The female wisely froze and lay still. The bloody male

awkwardly backed up, then crouched and put his head down.

She'd heard but ignored the words between Arvik and Nu'untivut. Now, she noticed waves of command from the shaman that wanted her to feel lost and alone, like the only one left in a cold and corrupt world, like nobody ever would or could love her because she was an abomination.

Dire-wolf rage flooded her. *Not happening, asshole.*

Moans and whines of distressed wolves came from all around. Nu'untivut apparently didn't care that he was hurting his own people, as long as he won. Double asshole.

She moved closer to the Ahklut male who smelled like Arvik but looked like a crippled old man. The stony gargoyle expression was familiar. Except for the hints of anguish in his eyes.

Ah, hell. Helping him was more important than the risk of being exposed as an interloper. Drawing from her wardrobe, she shifted to human.

The shaman's continued assault gave her an instant human stress headache. Arvik's amassed magical energy felt like static electricity on her skin. She edged closer to him anyway, using her magic to search for the wavelength he'd used when befriending Little Brother.

She became aware of quiet, distant music and flickering images, like a television in the next room. It felt familiar, like a movie she knew. Chills made the hair on the back of her neck stand up.

Obeying her intuition, she pulled off her glove and slipped her hand into Arvik's.

Colors, sounds, images, scents, and memories burst into her mind. The auction-house clinic. The hellfrog. Arvik's flurry of emotions when she'd kissed him. Older memories of people he'd found, loved, and lost, stretching back in time. His worry that she was deaf to his song. That

Nu'untivut was right, and he'd always be the hunted, hated monster.

She sent him an image of how she saw him. Noble, sneaky, funny, magical, sexy as sin. The man she'd been falling for since he'd chosen to help all the shifters escape. Since he'd shared his true nature with her. Since he'd smiled with admiration when he first saw her dire wolf. Since he'd chosen the much harder path of honesty, so they could be together.

I pledge you my heart. His unspoken words melted the last of the ice from Nu'untivut's despair magic.

She leaned closer, sending an image of their bodies entwined. *I lov—*

A simultaneous gunshot sound and blow to the ribs made her instinctively turn to block Arvik's body with hers.

She turned her head to see the sky-eyed native woman struggling to cock an old-style shiny nickel Colt .45 revolver.

Rayne drew two knives and spun quickly to throw one, all the while kicking herself for letting herself get distracted.

Nu'untivut's hand snaked out to catch the knife. He cocked his arm to throw it back, then howled in pain and dropped it, his glove charred and smoking.

Rayne's second knife hit the target, the shoulder of the shooter. She shrieked and twisted backward, stumbling away from the shaman. The gun flew out of her hand. She tripped over a rock and fell to her knees.

Nu'untivut shouted a string of words and spread his hands wide. A whirlwind of Arctic winds spun around him. In the blink of an eye, a blinding blizzard of gale-force winds expanded to engulf the Ahklut and the valley. The ground tilted and gravity went wonky.

The wind pressure tried to take her breath away.

Flailing, she reached toward the heat source that was Arvik, only to bash him in the nose.

He caught her arm and pulled her against him. Everything righted when he did.

I'm shielding the Ahklut from the worst of the storm, but I can't stop it. Nu'untivut is getting away.

A hazy image of the shaman shifting into wolf form and running south formed in her mind. She wrapped her arms around Arvik's strength. *Time to call in air support.* Her fingers tangled with her collar as she struggled to pull out the comms necklace.

She projected an image of a smart-ass grin, but wasn't sure it worked. *Since we're in a snowstorm, you could sing the Little Brother song to your new pack.*

20

Arvik gritted his teeth, trying to hang onto his magic. To his sanity. To his woman.

His shield protected the Ahklut against the worst of the Arctic hurricane, but each gust of magically produced wind felt like a sledgehammer on his head. Songs of the Ahklut swirled around him, demanding his regard.

Rayne mumbled into the pendant around her neck. A brief, brilliant flare of magic burst from her. Which made his body steal blood from his brain to send to his groin. The wolf and orca parts of him sang to the dire wolf part of her. *Battlefield!* he growled at them. *Dance later!*

Amusement bubbled up from her. She sent him a fleeting image of her as a stripper sliding sensuously on a pole. *This kind of dancing?*

Not helping. *No, I was—*

Subsonic thunder ripped through his brain. Wolf instinct said to run, to find a cave. A screech like rending metal vibrated his bones. Orca instinct said to dive deep and swim as far as his air lasted.

Thunderbirds. Flying death.

Long-ago memories seized him. His parents had saved him from their attack by sacrificing themselves.

Arvik! The magnetic voice compelled him to listen. An image pushed through his spiraling thoughts, one of the smiling sheriff from Kotoyeesinay. *You know him. He only wants Nu'untivut.*

He clamped his jaw tighter and fought his instincts. He did know the man. More to the point, he trusted his mate.

Her arms tightened around him. *Your pack's fear will kill them. Help them.*

She was right. Chaos and cacophony reigned, ripping them apart note by note.

Dredging up strength from somewhere, he sang. Charisma magic helped deliver his message of calm, of peace.

He soothed the bleeding wounds of loneliness that Nu'untivut had gouged into them all, singing of the vibrant community he'd discovered with his grandparents. Of his deep love for his mate. Of his hope that they could someday find the same happiness.

Another thunderbird screech sent a shiver through him and the Ahklut.

He sang of family and friends, and justice long overdue. Of his memories of his last days with the tribe, all those centuries ago. Of the deaths Nu'untivut had admitted to during the final confrontation.

The Ahklut shared their images of their cowardice and shame at how they'd been conned by the shaman's lies again. How they'd wanted to go south with the others today, but followed him when he went after Nu'untivut.

Arvik, look. Rayne's words in his mind sounded just like her voice.

Sometime during his songs, the magic had quit pounding

on his shield. Now the storm had mostly faded, leaving a blanket of fresh snow and ice on everything. The Ahklut had huddled closer together and closer to him. Some had shifted to human and were clinging to each other in pairs and trios.

Rayne pointed to the sky.

A giant gray and purple thunderbird from his childhood nightmares grappled with a squirming, clawing, biting Ahklut orca. The bird's paler chest bled from several wounds. The orca had dozens of slashes, and a bloody dark hole where an eye should be.

The thunderbird screeched. Arvik shivered, despite knowing he was safe. He leaned into the comforting songs sent by his Ahklut tribe. They were safe together.

Rayne made an exasperated sound. "Be right back." She disengaged from their embrace to stride toward the center of the tribe.

"Give me that!" Rayne pushed a huddled woman sideways and wrestled a Colt revolver from her hands.

Inyiqti flinched and hunched away, then cried out in obvious pain from the knife still stuck in her shoulder.

Rayne flipped open the revolver's load gate and tilted the gun to empty the bullets into her hand. She shoved them into separate pockets, then looked down at Inyiqti. "If I pull out the knife, will you behave?" The tone was stern, but not unkind.

Inyiqti looked up with wary suspicion, but nodded.

Healing magic blanketed Inyiqti as Rayne slowly extracted the knife. Tears streamed down Inyiqti's face.

Rayne stood and held up the knife. "These are keyed to me. If anyone finds the other one, don't touch it, or you'll get burned. Come get me." She used her pants to wipe the blood off the blade, then slid it into her wrist sheath.

A deafening cacophony of high-pitched screeching

overhead drew Arvik's attention. His eyes widened in astonishment.

Four desert dragons wearing what appeared to be puffy down vests flew just below the battling thunderbird and orca. A net stretched taut between the dragons.

The thunderbird opened his talons. The orca clawed at the air as he fell. His heavy body sank the center of the net. The dragons flew an efficient pattern to secure the top of the net.

The orca in the net shifted into the man. He rolled over fast. Magic flared. The net charred and broke.

The shaman fell, more magic flaring. A shimmering distortion appeared in the sky below him. He plummeted through it and vanished.

Arvik vowed to himself and his tribe to track Nu'untivut to the ends—

Unexpectedly, Rayne raised her fists in the air. "We win!"

She turned to smile at Arvik, then at the rest of the confused Ahklut. "I guessed you all might be blind to fairy rings, so I asked my genius magister sister to call some colleagues for backup." She pointed up toward the empty sky. The dragons were winging south with the net, while the thunderbird descended toward the north. "His evil ass just got sent on a thrill ride to a fairy demesne where Kotoyeesinay keeps prisoners."

Elder Tiri made her way closer, but stopped a respectful distance from Rayne. "We hear your song, Loup Blanc Apporte Hilaluktoq. You are now one of us."

"That's kind of you, but underneath all this finery"—she opened her jacket to examine a small dent in her armor —"I'm not just a *loup blanc*, a white wolf bringing something, I'm an Ice Age dire wolf. Are you sure you want one in your pack?" She poked her finger through the bullet hole in her jacket. "We tend to be trouble."

Old Uklaq barked a laugh. "We hear your song. You'll fit right in."

Tiri tilted her head toward Arvik. "May your union with the shaman Maq'arviqeriq be blessed."

Arvik blinked in surprise. "You know who I am?"

Tiri smiled. "Now we do. Not at first. Not until you healed people in need." She tilted her head toward the other elders. "The oldest of us remember what healing magic felt like. We remembered our place as elders and showed the others how to hear past the surface ice and listen." She made a dismissive sound. "The warriors ignored us. Nu'untivut listened to no one."

"He listened to me." Inyiqti climbed awkwardly to her feet. "None of you did." Her tone mixed accusation and deep hurt.

Arvik tried to see the source of her pain, but the oracle had the strongest song block of any Ahklut he'd ever met. He caught and held her gaze, and opened his heart. "I will listen."

Rayne moved back next to his side to take his hand. She turned to Inyiqti. "I will listen." Her expression softened. "When you're ready."

Arvik couldn't think of very many people who would extend such compassion to the person who'd shot her twenty minutes ago.

Soft tones emitted from Rayne's necklace. She touched it and flared magic. "You're on speaker with the Akhlut. Go."

"If you're done executing your own extracurricular war plan," growled an irascible Brooker, *"get your ass back to Fort LeBlanc. Bring Sheriff Tanner and your sister, so her mate doesn't shred me. Bring Díaz, too, if you didn't have to kill him. We've got*

about a hundred Ahklut prisoners, another four hundred who are asking for refuge, and even more who are calling themselves Ulu and wanting us to let them take the others to their tribal lands near Vancouver. The Fort LeBlanc elders have questions for you all."

Rayne laughed. "On our way, Shifter Tribunal Special Liaison Yada-Yada-Yada Brooker. We'll have some more refugees and a few more prisoners for you."

She deactivated and dropped the pendant, then moved closer to him. "I've got questions for you, too, Mr. Gargoyle, so don't you dare vanish again, or I really will find Lerro to hunt you down."

He reeled her gently into his arms. He knew he was to blame for the notes of loneliness and doubt that hid between her teasing words. "I am yours." His inner animals sent songs of their own to her. He sent a little healing spell her way, to erase the impact bruise underneath her armor.

She shivered against him. "Your magic always revs my engines. Unless you want me to jump you right here, let's get your people settled and find a place for us."

The sight of Arvik's cabin… Well, okay, the illusion that hid Arvik's cabin set Rayne's heart singing. He'd asked for time to "make things ready." She'd given it to him by running as a wolf for a couple of hours, exploring the territory. From the scent trails, Little Brother's pack hadn't been in the area for weeks. Unsurprising, since natural wolves needed big territories to keep themselves fed, and Arvik's porch made a poor winter den.

She'd used the time to reflect on the events of the last few days and to ponder what was to come. The Fort LeBlanc elders' big surprise battle plan had been the secret alliance with the Ulu, and their bold plan to convince the

Ahklut to join them instead of attack the town. She shivered at the thought of the terrible risks Arvik had taken, but she had to admit he was the only one who could have pulled it off. He was a special man. She wanted to come up with a way to convince Arvik to take her to visit the Pacific Northwest and his people. She'd like to meet them.

The rocks-and-downed-trees illusion faded to reveal Arvik standing in the cabin's doorway. She bounded down the snowy hill and leaped onto the porch. Shifting to human, she headed straight for his open arms.

Vivid images orchestrated with an emotional undercurrent—what the Ulu and Ahklut called a song— caressed her senses as much as the feel of him against her. The taste of his lips on hers.

Laughing, he pivoted her into the cabin's big room and shut the door. "You're all wet."

"Sorry. I chased a rabbit and ended up in a drift. It's only December, but the valleys up here are already full." She should have shaken the snow off before shifting.

Scents of food, of flowers, of wood all faded as the smell of him overwhelmed her. Nuzzling her nose under his shirt collar, she drew in his furry saltwater scent. "I'm rethinking our plan."

He raised her chin for a long, sensuous kiss. She had totally lucked out in finding a man who loved kissing and had five hundred years of experience doing it.

"Yes?" His short beard tickled as he kissed his way toward her ear.

Her nipples became aching points, demanding attention. She clutched his hips and pulled him close to revel in the hard bar of his arousal. "I've wanted you for so long. I don't want to wait until your people are settled, or the asshole shaman and warriors get judged, or the Shifter Tribunal decommissions me from the army. I don't even want to wait for your venison stew. Whether or not the mate magic happens, I love you. I want whatever time with you I can get."

He kissed her again, sending images of them together drenched in love. "I'm already yours. My grandmother says making love will form the bond. Are you sure you want to be mated to a hellfrog prototype?"

The controversial origin story had set off a firestorm among the Ahklut refugees, like it had once done with the Ulu.

Rayne smiled. "Hell, yes." She slid her hands under his loose shirt and traced the broad shoulder muscles with her palms. "Are you sure you want a dire wolf for a mate?"

"Top of my list." His wandering fingers explored her stiff nipple.

She arched into him. "Then let's go for the gold."

He walked her backward to the overstuffed chair near the window. She pulled off her T-shirt and tossed it, then helped him push his shirt off his shoulders.

The scent of his arousal mixed with hers, sending a shudder of desire through her. His beautiful brown skin, lighter than hers, and wide male nipples made her want to lick him all over. She sent him an image of that as she pushed off her sweatpants and kicked them aside.

He pulled a small packet out of his pocket and handed it to her, then high-stepped out of his jeans.

She laughed. "I love a man who's prepared." She sat on the arm of the chair and tore the packet open. "Bring me that glorious manhood so I can put this on you."

She wanted to take her time, exploring the shape and taste of him, find out what made him pulse, but neither of them could last if she did. Her trembling hands made it a challenge just to slip the condom onto his stiff shaft.

He stroked her hair and hummed softly. A picture blossomed in her mind of his sensual plans for her.

"Oh, yeah, all that, right now." Everything ached for him, even her magic. Golden mating-bond threads colored her vision as he helped her slide into the chair.

Words failed her the moment his mouth latched onto first one nipple, then the other. Thoughts disintegrated altogether by the time he got to her core and set her blood on fire.

Arvik went straight for her pleasure and was rewarded with the first of what he hoped would be a lifetime of her orgasms. He stayed with her spasming hips, using his tongue to draw a staccato series of short moans from her.

The burst of her magic may as well have been her hands caressing and stroking him. He gritted his teeth to keep control.

She pulled at his shoulders. "Inside." Her image left no doubt what she wanted. She pulled the thick throw pillows to support her back.

He expected the storm of sensation when he entered her, but not the sheer relief. Their mutual groans made a powerful song as he reached her depths. Time stopped as the moment etched his memory. Sweat made her skin shine like polished mahogany. Shifter magic seeping into her pores and his. Her legs around his hips the only thing holding him on the planet. His heart full to overflowing.

I love you, too. She sent him an imperative image. *Move!*

He started a slow rhythm, but soon lost it to the chaos of driving need. Supporting her with one arm for a moment, he grabbed her hand to put between them, encouraging her to stroke herself to another peak.

Tingling from the soles of his feet to the back of his neck spread to all of him. His magic reached for the golden threads of hers and wove together to create an unbreakable bond. He howled his body's pleasure as he slammed his hips hard against hers, jerking with release.

Through their new bond, her spasming bliss flooded him anew, making him gasp like a long-distance runner. He lifted her hips back onto the wide chair, then buried his face into the crook of her neck.

The bond sent tendrils of magic through him, filling gaps he hadn't even realized were there. Sometimes, shifter-mate magic resulted in a mingling of gifts. To keep Rayne, he'd take whatever the shifter's goddess gave him.

"Wow," she murmured. "That's gonna be hard to top." Her long, contented sigh tickled his ear. Amusement pulsed through their bond. "But I sure as hell want to try."

He lifted his head and gave her a lascivious leer. "Wanna come upstairs and see my condom collection?"

Hours later, he lay on his back with his divinely sexy mate sprawled on top of him, her head on his shoulder.

Whatever else the shifter bond had done, it had given him the ability to smell her true scent underneath the magic that modified and masked it. His own scent had permanently altered, too, into one similar to hers.

Desire still simmered in his blood, but they had days to work that out between them before life outside the cabin demanded their attention. Such as luring Aldenrud away from Fort LeBlanc to face the Shifter Tribunal before the auction-house owners got to him first. And tracking down the auction-house victims and their buyers.

He rubbed the muscles of her back, with long strokes

along the muscles under her shoulder blades. "Why don't you want Brooker to know you have the auctioneer's tablet with the sales records?"

She took a long breath and let it out slowly, then rolled off of him and sat up. "Short answer? I think they have a clue about what happened to my father. He was an agent for the Shifter Tribunal, investigating the auction house. I suspect someone in the Tribunal burned him, and he's a prisoner or a slave somewhere. The family tracking spell says he's dead, but my heart says otherwise."

He sat up to face her. "You don't trust Brooker? Or Myelle?"

She shook her head. "They're about the only two I do trust. But not their staff, or the politicians, or whatever other departments they have to deal with. The shifter-purity mess proved that. I have the unshakable feeling that I'll only get one chance to find my father alive." She sighed. "My father is no prize, but he's my father and Skyla's, and I know he'd go to the ends of the earth and beyond to rescue either of us."

He took her hand in his to kiss the back of it. "I can't think of a better honeymoon."

She raised an eyebrow. "Oh, so we're newlyweds, are we?"

He laughed. "We're better than that. We're true mates." He pulled her into his lap. "We're sneaky, crafty spies, and the only way the person who has your father will know we were there is because your father is suddenly missing."

She palmed his face, her eyes bright with tears. "I love you." The corner of her mouth raised in a crooked smile. "And if you tell me 'I know,' I'll shoot you."

His two inner animals took over and kissed her, stopping his stupid human self from saying exactly that.

Thank you for reading **Dire Wolf Wanted**. I hope you loved Arvik and Rayne, and how they worked through their past to build a future together.

If this is the first book you've read in the Ice Age Shifters series, you can catch up by reading SHIFTER MATE MAGIC, set in 1993 and featuring a big bear of a man and a woman who's had bad experiences with shifters, and SHIFT OF DESTINY, set in present day, and featuring a prehistoric lion shifter and a woman convinced there's no such thing as magic, or sexy shifters. HEART OF A DIRE WOLF, book 3, introduces the first dire wolf sister, her growly Siberian tiger mate, and the wondrous and mysterious sanctuary town of Fort LeBlanc.

If you love paranormal romance, check out In Graves Below, in the delightfully quirky worlds of Magic, New Mexico.

If space opera is your cup of tea, Earl Gray, hot, you could try Overload Flux, the first book in my Central Galactic Concordance series.

Sign up for my newsletter so you don't miss out on future books: bit.ly/CVN-news

Follow my Facebook page, CarolVanNattaAuthor, for exclusive insider news and sneak peeks of future books, both paranormal romance and space opera romance.